THESE GREEN FIELDS

978-0-9555314-1-5

Published by Causeway Publishing, Co Dublin
www.causewaypublishing.com
Printed by Gemini International Limited, Dublin 15
www.gemini.ie

For Martina

Prologue

The two boys sit huddled together on the carpet, fidgeting as they watch the action unfold on the screen in front of them. One of them taps a minute hurl on the floor, while the other rolls a sliotar round his fingers, both boys apparently hypnotised by the game. Their father gulps at a glass of Guinness on the sofa behind them.

Eddie Brennan fires a shot into the Limerick goal to push Kilkenny further in front and half of the crowd jump and scream in triumphant delight. The reaction in the living-room at first is muted, but after a few moments one of the little boys, he of the hurl, turns round to his father.

"Da, why do Mayo never play a final?"

"Well son, you know that's a very good question," replies his father.

The little hurler continues looking up at his father, and then realising there is no more to the reply he turns back to the game. His father takes another gulp of beer, but he is no longer concentrating on the television. His eyes glaze over as he gazes out through the rain-streaked window.

PART ONE

CHAPTER ONE
November

Con pounded the dark, compacted sand along the Atlantic shore, his unseeing eyes blind to the bank of dunes on the opposite side of the bay. His ears were deaf to the roar of the waves over the rocks, and the bare skin of his arms was unaware of the stinging of another petulant storm. This was his therapy, and it was his time alone with his lover. He only had eyes for the posts, only had ears for the crowd. He replayed the points from before, dreamt up the goals to come, felt again the thrill of victory and the pain of defeat.

And the other pain too. For nowadays his daily run was different.

His mind replayed the final moments, the images sharper than the rain, the shouts louder than the sea, the pain brighter and more brilliant than the storm light in the sky.

The knee gives way under the challenge. He feels it grating. Bone against broken bone.

The rain fell harder, the sea urged itself in and Con pushed himself on, ignoring his screaming lungs and his aching shins and the wild, wet hair stuck to his face. The light was fading, but he didn't need to see the route he had run every day for years. For years, until that day. The day he had been stopped in his tracks.

The metal strip of a hurl smashes his cheek under his right eye.

Until the end. Admittedly, he had already toyed with the idea of retiring, first from the county, then after a couple of years from the Kilbruagh club, but he wanted to do it gracefully and in his own time, not because the headlines on the back page of all the newspapers had him at death's door.

His hand on his face. He feels his cheek give way under his fingers.

After the first operation was hailed a success, his thoughts turned, of course, to a triumphant return to the team as soon as possible, so he had been shocked when first Deirdre, then his brothers, and finally Paddy Mac the bainisteoir and all his team-mates started to talk about his hanging up his boots. Had they lost the plot?

You could lose the sight in the right eye.

As it turned out he missed the rest of the championship, but he had spent those months arguing with all the people he loved the most about the future of his playing career, arguing until he was Dublin blue in the face, shouting at the deaf until finally nobody would listen any more. And the season ended without him. And the next season started without him. To top it all, his team had qualified for the Connacht club final without him.

Now that all the shouting was done he was determined to show everyone how wrong they were. So he pounded the beach alone, day after rainy day, until he could run for seventy minutes without wanting to die.

He ran the mile home at a light jog, gulping in the frozen evening air, keeping close to the dry stone walls yet maintaining a steady rhythm. He had been running these roads since childhood, and knew all of them as if they were his team-mates. He was living once more in the home he had grown up in, a whitewashed, low stone house with thick walls from more than a century before which had once been part of a farm, and although there was much less farming done since his grandfather's death, the place still had the outbuildings to reveal its former life.

After his father's passing, Con had watched his mother fade and had persuaded Deirdre that they should move her in with them and the kids. After all, in a new house they had the room. However, Con's mother had other ideas about who was moving where, and the new house had been sold, mercifully before the market started to collapse. Now his mother had passed too, but the family were happy in the old farmhouse and there was no question of moving them on again.

The pleasant calmness he always felt at seeing the lights of his house in the darkness under the trees faded as he spotted the car parked up the side of the barn. An old maroon Carina, battered from rocky Connacht fields and unforgiving Connemara roads. Paddy Mac the bainisteoir. He slowed to a walk then stopped at the gates to gather his thoughts. He breathed deep, smelling the intensity of the damp earth.

The last time they had spoken had been at the hospital on the day Con had been discharged. They hadn't spoken so much as shouted. In truth Paddy Mac was only angry about the injuries, and was worried that Con's determination to return could be his undoing if he took another knock without a helmet. Con couldn't see the preoccupation in his old bainisteoir's face – or maybe he didn't want to – but took it all as another attack against his wishes to carry on playing. A nurse had to come in to tell them to quieten down, but both men had blundered far too far into the red mist to be calmed down by some young lass in a uniform. They were rude to her, and then they carried on hurling abuse at each other.

You're a fucking coward. You're an old fool.

Eventually the nurse returned with the local female garda, who was there by chance visiting a relative, and she persuaded the men to take their fighting elsewhere. They didn't. They had said enough, and so they said no more.

Now the words echoed through Con's head, as they had done so many times before in that awful vacuum between turning out the light and falling asleep. As always when he lost his rag, Con was ashamed of his own behaviour, of his ranting and ravings, of the things he had said. But as always he was far too proud to go back on any of it or admit that he may have been wrong. Except that this time it was worse, because he could always say anything to his wife, but with this fight he hadn't even been able to admit to Deirdre that he had been wrong. Or apologise to her.

What the fuck would you know? You're just here to raise my kids.

THESE GREEN FIELDS

Inevitably it had hung in the air ever since that day, and although they had all left the anger behind in the hospital, the resulting hurt was still raw.

But here was the Carina. The cows had come home to roost.

The kitchen was warm from cooking and the smell of dinner hit Con in the face, even though the last thing he needed right now was food with his stomach in knots. He moved round the kitchen to the sink to wash his hands, all the while looking at the floor and refusing to acknowledge any of the people in the room. He took his time over his hands, found a tea towel and dried himself thoroughly, neatly folded the towel and placed it on the worktop by the sink, and then he turned slowly and leaned back against the edge of the worktop. He thrust his meaty hands deep into his pockets and studied the thick slabs of stone that made up the floor. He had done exactly the same all the way through his childhood every time he had been in trouble with his parents, and the habit had followed him into adulthood.

He finally deigned to glance up momentarily to confirm who was there, and saw to his surprise that Deirdre and Paddy Mac were accompanied round the solid oak table by Father Dónal, the ridiculously young priest from the local

16

parish church, and Seán O'Flaherty, the club captain. And nobody looked angry.

He looked at Deirdre, who stood up from the table and stared back with a mute plea in her eyes. *Just listen to them. Just talk to them.*

He owed her that much, so he looked Paddy Mac square in the face, pursing his lips as if to emphasise that it would be the bainisteoir who would have to break the silence. *You come to my house, you sit in my kitchen, you'd better have something to say.*

"How are you, O'Coolahan?" asked Paddy Mac.

"Grand, and yourselves?" replied Con.

"Aye." Father Dónal and Seán nodded replies but stayed silent. There was an obvious chronological order to this conversation, and everybody in the kitchen understood this. The bainisteoir chewed his lip for a moment before continuing. "You been training, so?"

"Running on the beach. I keep myself fit. Just in case. You know." He seemed to steel himself and jutted out his jaw. "For when I come back." He continued staring at the bainisteoir with a defiant glint in his eye. Paddy Mac held his gaze calmly, with no hint of resentment in his eyes.

"So you still want to come back then?" This was new.

"I do," replied Con, with caution in his voice. Again he pursed his lips; Paddy Mac would have to play the card before Con would commit himself to anything. However, it was Seán who spoke for him.

"We'd love you to come back, Con," he said, emphasising the simplicity of the statement with a shrug of his strong shoulders. It was almost as if he had not spoken, because Con ignored Seán and kept his eyes fixed on Paddy Mac's face.

"I want to hear that from you." A jut of the jaw. Crossed arms.

"We do, Con, we all want you back." The bainisteoir nodded with conviction and the look on his face revealed that he hoped he had injected the right amount of credibility into his voice. Con did not reply, but as he continued staring at Paddy Mac there was an almost imperceptible change in his stance as if he had relaxed a little. Deirdre, who had not moved from her position against the worktop, decided it was a good moment to refill the half-empty cups of tea. The three guests were grateful of the opportunity to escape from the intensity of the conversation for just a moment; they shifted in their seats and thanked Deirdre for the tea. Father Dónal had hardly even breathed since Con had come in, but now he felt confident enough to stretch out a bony hand and help himself to a biscuit

18

from the plate that sat forgotten in the middle of the kitchen table.

Con stared at the floor. All this was a bit sudden.

"Why now? You need me for the final, right?" He said this with conviction, absolutely certain that he was right.

Seán's face said otherwise. He leaned forward as if to answer, but glanced at Paddy Mac before speaking; the bainisteoir shrugged and nodded. Seán spoke.

"You see, a while back, it must have been this year's All-Ireland final now, my boy asked me a question that I couldn't answer. I couldn't give him an answer and that bothered me, and it's been bugging me ever since. We were watching the match, and he turned to me and asked me, Da, why don't Mayo ever play a final? And I couldn't tell him why."

"But we all know why, Seán, it's because there's no Connacht Championship. We've no way of qualifying for the All-Ireland. We're not going to get anywhere playing the Christy, even if we are getting better. What's this all about, Seán?"

"Well, I got to thinking and I had a talk with Paddy and we think we should talk to the Board about starting it all up again." He spoke fast, without taking a breath, as if he knew

19

how absurd the proposal sounded. Just as Seán had expected, Con laughed.

"Ah come on, Seán, ye can't be serious. That's a daft idea. And anyway, ye'll have to be quick about it, Galway are trying to get into Leinster."

"All the more reason why it has to be now. We have to have one more go at them before they trip off to the Pale."

Con laughed again, but this time at Seán's description of the east. "Anyway, when was the last time Mayo won a championship? Do we have any?"

"That's another thing, Con," interjected Paddy Mac. "Our last one was 1909. Virtually ninety-nine years ago. If we could set this up, it probably wouldn't be this next season it'd be the next year. 2009. A hundred years. It makes perfect sense."

"No, Paddy, it makes absolutely no sense at all, is what it makes. Galway are going to Leinster. Dublin will kick up a stink over it, but in the end they'll all vote yes. It makes sense to them. That's what makes sense, Galway and the Cats and Wexford getting more competition." Con stopped for a second and frowned. "And now I come to think of it, what part am I supposed to play in all of this?"

"Most capped Mayo player still playing," (he ignored Con's sarcastic snort) "most NHL goals of any Mayo forward;

you're a hero to the kids. If you spoke to the Board..." His voice trailed away as Con started shaking his head in protest.

"You can count me out of that one Seán; I'm not doing your dirty work for you just because you've got some hare-brained scheme your boy's put you up to." He was smiling in spite of himself. He had always had a great relationship with Seán, on the pitch and off it; Deirdre and Seán's wife Ciara were close friends and even the kids had always got on well, being of a similar age, and both men had made sure that their families had not been affected by the silence of the previous months. More accurately, Deirdre and Ciara had made sure that their husbands' silence had not affected the families in any way.

Seán smiled back at his friend. "Now, Con, it's not dirty work, but you know as well as I do that the Board will always listen to you." He paused, and then decided to take the plunge. "And although you won't admit it here, you know in your heart of hearts that you're well up for it. Teach them lot a lesson."

Con stared at the floor. Paddy Mac took a biscuit and munched along with the young priest. Seán threw a complicit wink at Deirdre who shot a subtle smile back at her husband's friend. They both knew that Con would be unable to resist the challenge. Especially if it meant coming back.

21

Suddenly Con pushed himself away from the sink and swept the plate of biscuits of the table.

"You know what? I can smell me dinner and I'm hungry. Ye've all got a cheek turning up here to try and rope me into some crazy plot against the neighbours. On yer way, the lot of ye!"

The bainisteoir and the captain took the hint; pride prevented any further conversation, but in their own way the men had started to heal the damage their own words had caused. Oblivious to the strong undertones of a unity reunited, the priest let his gaze follow the plate as it gracefully curved through the air before realising that the other two men had got up to go. He hurried to his feet too, wiped the crumbs from his lips and watched in timid embarrassment as Paddy Mac and Seán said goodbye to Deirdre with the ease of men who are comfortable with women.

Con saw the men out into the dark yard and shook their hands in silence. Each man looked in the eyes of the others to search for some last vestige of rancour, but found none. Like little boys whose arguments burn as fiercely as the summer sunset, they had settled their differences with little fuss.

However, there was one small doubt remaining in Con's mind. As he took the priest's fragile hand in his own, he squeezed hard and frowned down at the featherweight father.

"Just tell me one thing, Father. What on Earth are you doing here this evening?"

Father Dónal winced at Con's grip and stuttered a reply.

"Ah, well, you see, Con, these gentlemen thought they might not be so welcome in your house. You know, after everything. They were a little worried you might not be happy to see them. So they asked me to come along with them. You know. To keep the peace."

Con stared at the priest for a second then roared with laughter. Paddy Mac and Seán joined in, and Father Dónal managed a nervous laugh as he rubbed his hand. Con slapped him hard on the shoulder, almost bringing the priest to his knees.

"Thank the Lord, Father that you're always around to offer your protection! I'm away to me dinner! Oh, hang on. What about that final, then?"

Seán shot a smile back over his shoulder as he climbed into the passenger seat of Paddy Mac's Carina.

After dinner, Deirdre cleared the plates into the dishwasher while Con made a pot of tea, then she sat down opposite him and watched him carefully. She had never had a problem with his going back to the club; for all she cared he could hurl until he was eighty, as long as he did not kill himself in the process. There was only one thing she wanted from her husband, and if she knew her man at all he would face up to his responsibilities. More than anything she trusted her own judgement enough to know that she had married the right man.

Con sipped his tea and stared at the table. The solid wooden table top was pockmarked and burned, scarred and cracked along the grain. It was a well-worn map of the adventure of their marriage – the fights, the kids, the quiet moments when nothing else existed outside their own boundaries and the rest of the world faded away into the mist of a shared bottle of wine. More importantly, that table had sat in that kitchen for decades and was as much a part of the family as any person had ever been. His parents had laughed and cried around it too, and their advice about marriage and the sacrifices it entailed echoed inside his head as his eyes focused once more on the room.

He looked up to find Deirdre watching him with that face that women do perfectly – no sign of emotion, no approval or anger, simply a blank canvas waiting for a man to fill in the gaps with the right comment, or the wrong one.

He reached across the table and took her hand. Her expression did not change, but she continued to gaze at him.

"I'm sorry love. About what I said. None of it was true, I was just angry. You're much more important to me than that. I couldn't do any of this without you. I'm sorry."

He had looked back down at the table, almost embarrassed at the outward expression of emotions that he normally kept wrapped up in a very safe place, but the silence that came from his wife made him look up again. She stared at him for a few more agonising moments, and then she got up and came round the table to stand next to him. She stroked his cheek and whispered "I forgive you" in his ear.

That particular conversation was closed forever, and he had his biggest fan back on side.

CHAPTER TWO

The echoing clatter of studs on concrete flooded out of the door of the tiny makeshift building that housed the dressing rooms as the players trooped along the narrow corridor and out into the freezing evening air. As each player reached the threshold he broke into a trot and crossed the chalk line onto the pitch. They ran through white plumes of their own breath and fired slíotars at each other across the grass, spreading out and hitting longer and longer shots until they were within shooting distance of the posts. Some of them had a go, and derisive laughter or ironic cheers greeted the worst efforts.

THESE GREEN FIELDS

Paddy Mac and Seán were the last two out onto the pitch. They let the players run for a few minutes while they laid out plastic markers and discussed what they would do with the training session. When they were ready to start, they called the players into a group to stretch, joining in as the men pulled cold unwilling muscles into submission.

"Two laps, off ye go!" shouted Paddy Mac when he was satisfied the team had limbered up enough to ward off the threat of injury. Amid cheerful pissing and moaning the players set off on a jog round the perimeter of the pitch.

Con pulled up in the car park, killed the engine and sat in the sudden silence left behind by the music. He had wanted this so badly that now he was on the cusp of achieving the thing that had obsessed him for so long he was unsure how to feel about it. He knew he should feel happy, but truth be told he was more nervous than anything else. How would the lads react? More importantly, did he still have the skill to compete? He had heard stories of serious injuries finishing careers, not because of the physical effect on the player's body, but because of the psychological effect on the person. A subconscious fear creeps in, something subtle and undetected until the player ducks out of the first serious tackle. Would he be scared now?

Only one way to find out. He jumped out of the car, grabbed the bag and his hurl from the back seat and headed into the dressing rooms. He met no-one on the way in, and he took his time as he savoured once more the thick cocktail of damp walls and muscle spray. There was no other smell on Earth like this one to evoke a memory. No other smell, not silage, not his wife's perfume, described who he was with as much brutal eloquence as the smell of the dressing rooms before a game.

He sat alone on the slatted wooden bench and rattled his studs on the hard floor. A surge of energy was running through his legs, as if the exclusive ground of the dressing room was welcoming him home. He picked up the hurl from the bench and laid it across his knees, running his hands along the smooth shaft of ash. The time had come to stop complaining and play.

He strapped his helmet on and walked down the corridor and out into the floodlit night. The players were coming over from their two laps and were gathering round Paddy Mac for the next instructions. The bright light above the dressing room door blinded the players, so at first they could not see who was approaching them. As Con came closer, however, there were gasps of surprise.

"Con!"

"How you doing, man?"

"Hey Con, you've come back!"

Con stepped into the middle of the group and hugged a couple of players self-consciously, acknowledging the slaps on his helmet with a raised hand. The mood had lightened noticeably, and secretly Con was relieved that his return had warranted no more fuss than a few slaps on the back. Paddy Mac was pleased too, but he could not afford to let the players get into a party atmosphere too early in the evening.

He was about to get the team back into the mood for training when a loud roar made him turn round towards the car park.

"Con! You're back, man!"

All the players started laughing as a huge slab of a man struggled over the white fencing and ran over to the group, stripping off his tracksuit top and trying to dig his gloves out of his bag at the same time. Pádraicín, the goalkeeper, late as usual. As he arrived he attempted to hug Con but succeeded only in smacking his helmet with the hurl in his hand and almost flattening him. The team laughed harder as the goalkeeper finally succeeded in bear-hugging Con.

"Get off! Ya big mullock ya!" shouted Con as he tried to extricate himself from the lock.

"Hey Pádraicín, how did you get that black eye?" asked Seán as he stepped closer to examine the goalkeeper's bruised face. The big man glanced down uncertainly and looked at his legs.

"The other day I was in a hurry getting dressed. I tried to put me trousers on going down the stairs." He looked back up at the players with a sheepish smile as they exploded with laughter. Paddy Mac decided it was time to step in at last.

"Right, enough messing about. Pick a man, each one on one side of the pitch, practise yer long balls. Drop the slíotar, twenty push-ups. Go!"

The players paired up and started knocking the ball backwards and forwards across the pitch. There was enough distance between each player on the sidelines to make conversation difficult, and Con was perfectly happy with that. There would be time enough afterwards for anything that had to be said. He had avoided the club since the injury, and he had even taken to driving different routes so as not to drive past the place. Stupid, maybe, but when a person feels that strongly about something the reaction often appears extreme to outsiders. He had, of course, bumped into some of the lads around the town, uncomfortable muttered greetings in shop doorways. Typical bloody-minded men, they had not had the gumption to say the right things to each other. Apparently 'better out than in' only applied to trapped gases. The network of wives had kept everyone sane by constantly repeating the mantra of 'it's only a matter of time; let him get it out of his system'. Funny though, now they were all back together, there was probably nothing that needed saying.

An hour and a half of knocking the ball and each other round the pitch with more gusto than Paddy Mac had seen in recent competitive matches and the session was over. They said goodnight to the bainisteoir, grabbed their belongings from the dressing room and threw them into the boots of the cars in the car park, and then they walked the two hundred yards down the road to The Lawless, bleating and pucking each other and looking for all the world like a herd of unruly goats blocking the way.

According to local folklore The Lawless had stood on the same site since Queen Medbh was a princess. The pub had been in the Lawless family for the length of human memory and successive landlords were fond of saying that the surname was the most apt name for a local public house, for it really was a place where the ideals of local justice were enforced by the interested parties, through endless arguments and occasional fights. However, the people from the surrounding area also stated that the name of the pub was appropriate because the regulars – especially the local GAA team – were a bunch of hooligans.

31

Tuesday and Thursday evenings were often quiet in The Lawless until the players came in from training. The club's own bar had burned down the previous year, and until they got round to rebuilding it the closest pub was the regular haunt of both players and fans. The players always came in after training for a quick one, and to either dissect the previous weekend's debacle or prepare the following weekend's conquest.

They greeted the two auld fellas at the bar, ordered drinks and stood in a rough circle next to the bar. Every night the same story, standing is better than sitting because if we sit down now we'll be in here all night so if we stand up we'll only have the one. Every time the plan failed, and with Con back in the fold there was no evidence that this time would be any different.

Everyone had pints in their hands, even the drivers. There would be a few phone calls to wives come closing time. The wives were used to it; it was no different to dropping off a carful of kids and smelly kit to various houses, and they took it in turns the same way.

There were toasts to Con, then to the absent Paddy Mac, then to Pádraicín for actually nearly being early, and then a few more uncomfortable muttered comments about Con's return. Soon enough the conversation turned to Seán's boy and his question about Mayo. Until now Seán had only mentioned it to the bainisteoir and to Con, so the rest of the team was fascinated to hear about Seán's crazy idea about taking Galway on again after so long.

"They'll not hear of it, boy," stated Liam Murphy, a midfielder from deepest Cork, a place so deep that it figured on no map. His parents had had to move to Ballina for work when Liam was only a baby, and somehow his parents' accents had prevailed over twenty-five years of being a local Mayo boy. "They're off to Leinster, anyhow," he added with finality. There were murmurs of agreement.

"But that's exactly the point," replied Seán, "that's why it has to be now. One last game at least, for old times' sake if for nothing else." The players all pulled faces and thought about the possibility of pulling off one last victory over the old enemy. Most of the faces seemed to express that it would be difficult, if not impossible. Liam voiced the problem that occupied most of their thoughts.

"Who'll tell the Board, then?" More murmurings. "Ye'll never convince that bunch of aul' wans."

"We'll work out the details first, and then we'll approach them," said Seán. "You never know, maybe they'll go for it."

"You know, they never should have got rid of the championship in the first place," said Liam.

"Sure they couldn't let it carry on, Liam, it was a farce. It was a one-donkey race," replied fellow midfielder Niall O'Byrne. "What was the use to Galway of playing the same predictable match year after year? They'd won forty-odd times, Sligo and Leitrim never."

"True, but it was only in their interests to get rid of it. That's how they're ending up in Leinster," put in Pádraicín.

"But still, you can't just get rid of a Provincial Championship like that. That's no reason at all, just having one team dominating all the time. If that was enough of a reason, they'd just give it to Cork every year, boys!"

The other players laughed at his suggestion, and he replied with a look of mock hurt that they should doubt the Rebels' superiority. However, Con followed his argument.

"You know, he's not wrong though. If that was the case, they'd give Sam to Kerry and Liam to Kilkenny, and be done with it. I mean they're not that stuck up that they don't want to play the rest of us, but you ask a Kerryman who the best football team is, and he'll tell you."

"Well, the same as Dublin or Tyrone, or us for that matter, Con," replied Seán. "And Cork or Limerick or Waterford would all claim to be the best at hurling. Things

34

change, counties come and go, teams go in cycles, and everyone deserves a chance to beat whoever. Look at Kilkenny now, they've just won their second in a row, and they surely look good for a couple more, but nobody's won three in a row since Cork in the seventies. Clare, Wexford, Offaly, they've all won it recently enough, so it makes it worth it to have the championship because you never know."

"But that's exactly the point, lads," persisted Niall, "there's five counties here, two have never won the championship, two have won it once before our grandfathers were born and Galway have won the other six hundred times. That's not just three in a row, now, lads, that's taking the mickey. They've been permanent champions for nearly a century."

"All the more reason why we have to beat them!" declared Pádraicín to roars of approval from the rest of the team.

"Well said, Pádraicín, and by the way it's your round!" said Con to more laughter. "Mine's a pint, so!"

Jackie Lawless had already seen a few empty glasses and had been setting out full ones on the bar top, so Pádraicín started ferrying them over to tables. With an air of comical resignation the players made themselves comfortable round the tables and toasted Pádraicín's abilities as a waiter.

Seán continued with the arguments in favour. "Look, if they want competition, what better way for us to improve than by being able to play matches. A couple of matches a season isn't enough. And anyway, if the problem is lack of quality, well there's those that'd argue that Leinster football is not up to much. When was the last time a Leinster county won anything? But nobody would dare suggest changing anything there. Although everyone's talking about the Laois and Westmeath hurlers running off to Ulster because they feel pushed out already."

Con joined in again too. "You know, I'm surprised nobody's mentioned Ulster." There were murmurs of agreement. "I mean, there was slightly more competition there, mainly because there are more counties, I know, but at the end of the day Antrim had won thirty-odd titles too when they decided to stop playing. They didn't play it for forty years, and now it's come back stronger than ever, and not because of the absence either. It's strong because the other teams are being given the chance to play."

"Well, there's other factors too, Con," argued Niall. "And anyway, since they started saying it's being played again it's only really Antrim and Down, and Antrim have been running away with it like they always did."

"Not so, Niall," replied Liam. "Down and Derry have both had a look-in, and even New York got to the final too. And of course this year it's all nine counties. And on top of that, even though Antrim are going to join Leinster too, they're still playing the Ulster championship to give it credibility. Galway shouldn't just back out like that."

"You know what, though, lads," interjected Ger Flynn, Con's fellow forward and childhood sparring partner, "this game wouldn't be a bad thing for another reason too. If we could start this thing up again with Galway gone to Leinster we could have a competitive championship every year. The quality might not be very high for now, but at least we could start somewhere instead of watching the rest of the country play while we sit idle."

"Never spoke a truer word, Ger!" laughed Con. "That's fighting talk alright!"

The pints turned into rounds and the ideas got grander. By the end of the barrel Mayo were All-Ireland champions and they had all but solved all the world's problems. There was still one question unresolved, however, and now all eyes were on Con.

Finally tiredness, the beer and a feeling of goodwill towards his teammates decided the matter for him.

37

"Go on then, I'll go and speak to them, so. But Seán's coming with me."

CHAPTER THREE

It was not often that Con dressed up at all, but he felt that the occasion warranted a jacket. No tie, now, he had to draw the line somewhere, he certainly did not want to end up looking like some old bank manager, but a jacket and a shirt was a smart enough combination. Deirdre smiled to herself as she watched her husband look at himself uncertainly in the big mirror in the hall. She thought he looked fantastic but she knew her man well enough to keep her thoughts to herself. No need to put him off.

Seán arrived promptly and beeped outside. When Con left the house and crossed the yard to the car Seán shot him exaggerated looks of shock through the windscreen. As his friend opened the door and climbed in, the captain laid into him.

"Would you look at yerself! Are you getting married again or something? Does Deirdre know? It's only the Board, nobody special."

"Feck off, I want to make a good impression with them. I have to, after everything that's happened. I reckon they'll want their pound of flesh after the things I've said about them."

"Sure, they'll be glad to see you back. Just smile nicely and everything will be alright." He pulled out of the yard and onto the road. "They're at Connolly's house."

"Who's there?"

"Dunno."

Con winced inwardly. He hated Connolly more than either of the others, from his pretentiously columned house to his self-importance. Everyone knew the money was his wife's, what nobody knew was how she put up with a dopey bollocks like him. He was so boring he even had elbow patches in his speech but he was vindictive in the extreme when it came to getting one up on somebody else. The news that they were going right into the wolf's lair dampened Con's good mood and they drove in silence back towards the end of the bay.

Connolly's house stood on a rise overlooking the length of the bay, one of a group of exclusive houses built during the housing boom. It was a large low house, decorated in soft, peachy orange paint with a darker colour round the window frames like the smudged lipstick on the girl stood too long at the dance. His Mercedes, her Chelsea tractor and their eldest's Imprezza with more accessories on the outside than on the inside stood in front of the house, while a toppled kiddy-sized GAA goal and a Japanese fountain in bog black and sky grey decorated the grass to the side. Seán parked on the gravel next to an old Ford and jumped out of the car, giving Con no time to ready himself. No deep breaths.

Connolly's wife Kathleen answered the door and showed them into the conservatory at the back of the house. Kathleen was elegant in middle age and exuded a sense of calm which belied the ferocity she showed in defending her clients. She had married just to have children and had found herself a man who had three kids in him and no personality. She wore the trousers even when she wore a skirt.

Kathleen left them to the beautiful views of the bay and went back to her study. Both men knew that Connolly would want to make what he thought of as an entrance, and sure enough he kept them waiting a full five minutes before making an appearance. Meanwhile Seán tried to make conversation, but Con was too unsettled to want to talk. He stared unseeing at the violence of the flowery patterns on the cushions.

Finally the door to the conservatory opened and in walked Connolly. He was a slight man, shorter than most, with a horrendous comb-over and sniper eyes. Behind him were the two other selectors, and Con was relieved to see Jimmy Dennehy and Mickey Joyce, the two oldest selectors. Connolly might strut about as if he was important, but these two were heavyweights who could tell him to shut up whenever they wanted. At the end of the procession came Connolly's little girl, carrying a grown-up tea set with the intense concentration of the child who wishes to please.

The men greeted each other with the civility of people who know they should shake hands before coming to blows and settled into the cushioned wicker chairs. Tea was poured, biscuits offered and rejected. Con decided to take the bull by the horns.

"Look gentlemen, first off I'd like to apologise for anything I may have said to offend you. I was just angry, that's all."

Connolly leaned back in his seat and opened his mouth, but the soliloquy was cut short before it began by Mickey Joyce.

"Thank you Con, that's very nice of you. We all accept the apology." He did not look at Connolly, but if looks could kill Connolly's raven-like eyes would have struck him dead. Jimmy Dennehy took the baton before Connolly could get a word in.

"So Seán, what did you want to ask us?"

Seán was as surprised as Con at the way the conversation had started, but he was not going to invite trouble by going down that road, so he pushed on with the real reason for the visit. Con was right behind him too; if he was reading the atmosphere right, this conversation might be easier than he had hoped.

"Well, it's a long story really, and ye know, most of it's not relevant, so in a nutshell, well, we'd like to have another go at the neighbours before they up sticks and cross the country."

Jimmy Dennehy's eyes widened in surprise. "Let me get this right. You want to play Galway. At hurling. One last time." He glanced at Seán for confirmation. Seán nodded. "Now then, is what you're saying that you'd like the championship to be held again? Because that's a big ask, Seán. We'd have to get the other counties involved, and the Provincial Board, and then there's Croke Park." He paused to let the effect of the last two words sink in. "And think of the money involved. And it's hardly as if we're in a position to push for that. Every season we think there could be an improvement and every season we're back where we started. We would need to be in a much stronger position at county level before we could think about asking for that."

Seán and Con nodded their agreement at the weight of the selector's argument and exchanged glances of compliance with Mickey Joyce. Connolly sat and quietly seethed. What could have been a show of strength in his mighty fortress by the bay had swiftly turned into an exercise in emasculation.

Jimmy Dennehy had let the words have their intended effect, and now the baton was returned to Mickey Joyce. "You know, lads, it's no bad idea asking Galway for one last go before they piss off on us. I don't reckon the other counties'd mind too much, there's not the same, shall we say, relationship between them." The players chuckled their agreement and waited for the old man to continue. He leaned forward and his eyes twinkled. "Now if you're talking some sort of unofficial match, honorary match – charity match, even – then you may be on to something. If we keep it local and don't bother Croke Park with it, all the better. As for it counting as a championship match, I don't reckon we'd get away with that without getting the other counties involved, and as I say, that would be difficult now."

He sat back and watched the two players from under fierce ash-grey eyebrows. Seán and Con glanced at each other; they knew that the man was talking sense, and neither of them was so interested in the issue to want to make a crusade out of it. It was only Galway, after all. They looked round at the selectors and nodded their agreement again. Jimmy Dennehy spoke.

"I have just one question for ye, lads. Who have you spoken to about this?"

"So far, just among ourselves at the club, and that only last week," replied Con.

"Good. Let's leave it at just that for now, will we? This'll take a bit of time, and we don't want anyone getting wind of it and blowing it up before we've even started, do we now?" More nods. "Alright, so. For now we'll see how the results go and then we'll have a look at it. Thank you for coming boys."

Con and Seán stood up quickly, shook hands all round and made their escape, one relieved that there had been no repercussions and the other amazed that the conversation had gone so smoothly. They left behind two men with the seeds of a plan, and another who was trying to remember the last time that he had gone through an entire conversation and not had the chance to say a word.

As they drove away, Con and Seán tried to replay the whirlwind conversation in their heads. Con puffed out his cheeks and let out a huge sigh.

"What's up, man?" asked Seán.

"Well, first up I can't believe I didn't get any more abuse than that. Secondly, did you see how those two had Connolly gagged? What was that about?"

"No idea, but it was strange alright. And I don't think he was expecting it either, from his face."

Con laughed. "Yeah, his face was a treat alright. Why do you think they did it, though?"

"For you, probably," said Seán, glancing over towards his passenger. "I reckon everyone wanted you back really. It's just that they were all worried about another knock to the head. They wanted to see you out for long enough to recover properly, and now they want you back. As for Connolly, maybe they wanted you to see that there were absolutely no hard feelings, and they weren't going to let that bollocks show you any. And, you know..." His voice trailed off, uncertainty taking over.

"You know what, Seán?" prompted Con, watching his friend's face carefully.

"Well, you'd already mentioned yourself about retiring. You probably don't have that much time left anyway. Maybe they wanted it all to finish on a good note rather than on a sour one." He threw in a non-committal shrug for good measure.

Con pondered this one. It was true he had thought about retirement from the panel, and maybe he had even voiced the thought on occasions – always half in jest, of course – but right now he really did not want to think about it. He had only just come back after months of being sidelined. Now was the time to think about more exploits on the pitch. He would obviously be back in the club side pretty fast – and with the postponed Connacht final coming up it was perfect timing – but even if he made the county panel they probably would not get very far in the League so that would mean no more games for the county until the following season.

A possible match against Galway would be even more important to him now.

CHAPTER FOUR

December

Chill winds blew the month of December in, but the floods that had prevented the Connacht club final from being played had fortunately stayed away. In Mayo the buzz was about Con's timely return to the Kilbruagh side; in Galway this news was either deemed irrelevant or spoken about in private. As far as Galway champions Kinglen were concerned, nothing was going to stand in their way of a fifth consecutive title and yet another shot at the All-Ireland.

The main stand of Pearse Stadium was full of fans, the vast majority sporting the maroon of Kinglen on scarves and hats. Small pockets of red and white Kilbruagh supporters could be seen among the crowd. Very few maroon seats were left unused. The terraces were mainly populated by young lads who had not come to the game as part of families; these lads stretched themselves out, smoking and laughing and enjoying the craic.

The day was blustery, with the adolescent mood swings typical of the cusp between Irish seasons. Clouds flew across the sky, the sun played hide and seek and the storm-like quality of the light persisted in headache-inducing intensity. The brightest periods of sunshine, accompanied by the biggest stray spots of rain, were enough to remind anyone that may have forgotten that the weather could turn in an instant if it so desired.

The wind was good for one thing, and that was keeping flags and banners alive in a constant stiff salute. As the players poured out onto the pitch for the anthem, the flags danced and waved in greeting and the atmosphere in the stadium rose in anticipation. The crowd did justice to Amhrán na bhFiann, while the players fidgeted like wild animals, their eyes intense and unfocused.

The anthem finished and a crescendo of noise washed the players around the pitch as they gave each other final shouts of encouragement and took up their initial positions. Con checked his helmet strap for the umpteenth time as he glanced over at Seán, who nodded back at him with an expression filled with the gravity of a gladiator. Con turned the other way and caught the eye of Liam and Niall in midfield, and the half-line trio of Dermot Reilly, Paddy O'Brien and Paul O'Connor. Their eyes said they were ready. In the distance Pádraicín prowled along his goal line, his broad shoulders hunched over and one meaty hand wrapped round his hurl.

Throw-in, and Ger Flynn jumped with the Kinglen player to challenge for the slíotar, the hurls clash and the ball falls at their feet, both players swinging at the ball on the ground, the Kinglen player connects and the slíotar flies into the Kilbruagh half where Niall O'Byrne flicks it up deftly with the end of his hurl and effortlessly sends it forty metres to where left half-forward Brian Lynch has surged into the Galway half, Lynch is challenged but takes the ball cleanly, looks up and sees the posts and takes the point. One-nil to Kilbruagh.

The smaller part of the crowd cheered the first blood and the flags waved, but the Kinglen fans responded with louder cheering and drowned out the fans from Mayo. The sun came out again and the crowd smiled and urged the teams on.

The points went backwards and forwards, each team taking turns to lead by one or two, but with neither being capable of pulling away. As the half went on, the forwards proved their accuracy, with only a couple of wides for each side. It would take something special to separate the sides, but it seemed that the first half would remain a fairly even affair. Little by little though, the frustration at not being able to shake the opponent off was leading to stronger challenges.

Twenty-five minutes gone, Kinglen leading by one, nine-eight, no goals so far, Kilbruagh have the ball in their half, left corner-back Dónal Branagh forward to left half-back Paul O'Connor, on to Niall O'Byrne in the midfield, inside the Kinglen half now, Kilbruagh maintaining possession but the Kinglen men pushing all the time, challenging every ball, trip, that's a foul inside the Kinglen half, no time to breathe or regroup as Seán O'Flaherty takes it quickly, up to left corner-forward Kieran O'Dwyer who's run inside the thirteen-metre line, he takes the ball beautifully in the air and with no apparent effort sends it high between the posts to even the scores.

The crowd were enjoying the game, especially the fact that points were coming thick and fast with very few wides, and the intensity on the pitch was felt keenly around the stadium. There had been no attempts on either goal; the players seemed content to keep securing points and certainly did not want to lose a scoring opportunity and perhaps fall too far behind. The tackles were flying in as fast as the points now too, and the referee had already had to speak to three players.

Just three minutes left of the first half now, Kinglen leading yet again by just the one point, this has been an excellent game so far, very accurate both forward lines, neither side able to pull away though, very intense the tackling, now Kinglen have the ball and are moving it around well, from the midfield to the half-forward line, they keep pushing forward, but the passes are shorter now, perhaps they are looking for the sting of a goal before the break, playing inside the forty-five, nobody is going for the posts, they are looking for a goal, inside the Kilbruagh twenty-metre line, thirteen metre-line, the forward shoots, that's an excellent save from Pádraicín Kavanagh, that's an excellent save indeed, he's just saved a certain goal there, that was definitely inside the post, he'll hang on to that for a second and just slow it down now, that'll be half time in a minute, but what an excellent chance went begging there for Kinglen, the shot was perfectly weighted towards the top corner and they could have gone in a goal and a point up, four points up but Kavanagh in the Kilbruagh goal threw himself across the square to meet that ball and he's made an important save there, that's half time and Kinglen are leading by a single point, a high-scoring half sees the men from Galway leading twelve-eleven.

The rain started at half time, light but relentless, the thin rain that soaks everyone and everything. The fans in the stand huddled together as the wind blew sheets of misty water in under the roof, and on the terraces the young lads hugged themselves under thin jerseys and gave up trying to light the next cigarette.

The sky darkened ominously as the players filed back out onto the pitch with noticeably less enthusiasm than at the start of the game. It was as if the weather was determined to win a battle with the players' morale, the black clouds sucking the enjoyment out of the match. Throw-in and the game started up again where it had left off, with strong tackles and even less quarter given than before the interval. A nasty cross-wind picked up too, and now for all their previous exploits the forwards found themselves fighting against the elements to get the ball between the posts.

However, the weather meant nothing five minutes into the second half when the match was turned on its head.

No score so far this half, that wind's playing havoc with the forwards now, even the longer passes are going astray, that's Niall O'Byrne with the ball attempting to surge forward into the Kinglen half, he's nearly within shooting distance, this could be the first point of the half if he can wait for a lull in the wind, he's not a classical forward but nevertheless O'Byrne is lethal from there, but that's a foul, surely that's a deliberate trip, that's a deliberate foul, he was already pulling O'Byrne's shirt then he tripped him with the hurl, he's fairly hacked at his ankle and brought him down, quite a shocking foul really, but the referee's given nothing, the minority Mayo support are certainly making themselves heard now, the Galway supporters stay silent, they know that was a foul, but look, as three Kilbruagh players try to catch up with the referee to remonstrate with him Kinglen surge forward now, the ball's inside the thirteen, the Kilbruagh defence has jumped overboard and that's a goal! That's a goal! Kinglen have scored, and they took advantage of the absence of the Kilbruagh defence who had gone to join in with the argument with the referee, Branagh had run over to the sideline to have a go at the linesman too, Kavanagh was left with no chance in the Kilbruagh goal as the forward crossed the thirteen-metre line he saw his spot in the bottom corner and Kavanagh couldn't get himself down in time with no-one challenging the Kinglen forward, and all the Kilbruagh players are around the referee now, you have to say that's a really silly thing to do, you can't just give up on the game like that when you're defending an attack, if you want to go and speak to the referee afterwards fair enough, but they abandoned ship at the worst

54

moment and that's put them a goal and a point behind, and Kilbruagh may now pay dearly for their anger and look! Conor O'Coolahan, their talisman and hero, is off! As captain Seán O'Flaherty was trying to drag him away from the referee, trying to drag him and three other players away from the referee while simultaneously trying to argue his point too, I don't know what was said there but something was said, the referee had waved them all away but something was said and the referee has turned back and pulled out the card! Well, well, what a dramatic explosion in the match and now Kilbruagh are four points down, they're a player down too and all of a sudden they look in complete disarray and you have to say that now this match is for Kinglen's taking.

The crowd had gone wild, the maroon half for the goal and the red and white sector for the foul and Con's sending off. Down on the pitch the Kilbruagh players were lost, looking around wildly as if to find the thread of the game that had been irreversibly cut right in front of their eyes. They did not know whether to carry on playing or to carry on arguing with the referee. Their concentration was shot to pieces and the burning sense of injustice had replaced the fire they had been playing with to the detriment of their game. Kinglen had them where they wanted them now and they could go in for the kill.

Sure enough for the rest of the half Kilbruagh were hanging off their opponents' shirt tails as point after point went over almost without reply. Kilbruagh failed to score for the next fifteen minutes and when they did, the difference between the two sides was so great as to make the point totally irrelevant. By the last five minutes the Mayo team had all but given up, and when a Kinglen forward again invaded the Kilbruagh thirteen the defence stood and watched in impotence as the back of the net rippled.

The final whistle could not come soon enough, and as the Kinglen players and their fans celebrated the 2-19 to 0-13 win, the Kilbruagh players sat in a disconsolate huddle in the middle of the wet pitch, as far away from the celebrations as possible. As the Galway rain grew heavier, each man wondered whether he would ever be able to pick up a hurl again.

Trophy, medals, the usual. The team couldn't be bothered with the circus around them. They watched the winning team through disdainful eyes, sick to the stomach as someone else picked up Kilbruagh's medals, Kilbruagh's trophy, the trophy all the Mayo men had picked up in their waking dreams every day for a month.

After saluting their patient, long-suffering fans, the Kilbruagh players filed into the dressing room and dropped down onto the wooden benches which lined the white plaster walls. Con was sat in a corner, his head in his hands. He did not look up when his teammates came in. He did not want to look at them and see the recrimination in their eyes. *Con lost it again. Shouted at the ref. Again.* He did not want to see the pain of defeat in their eyes because it would mean acknowledging his own pain. He was deaf to the clatter of studs and the dropped hurls and ripped Velcro on helmet straps and fingerless gloves. He felt nothing until a hand landed on his shoulder. He moved his hands away from his face and his body swayed to one side like a bridge whose supports have collapsed. As he steadied himself he glanced up and recognised Seán from his gloves. He immediately looked back down at the floor.

"What did you say to him, Con? I didn't quite catch it."

Con knew it was better to face the music now and get it over and done with. It would be no good trying to resolve the issue later, because once they all left that dressing room, once they all showered even, there would be no going back. Once the muck was washed off, the other muck, the invisible stain of anger would still be there. The damage would be done and it would weigh them all down silently until the next disagreement, when it would come roaring back to take a swipe at them all.

"It wasn't so much what I said to him, it was what he said to me first," said Con, looking up and glancing round at the players slumped on the benches.

"Well? What did he say then?" prompted Niall.

"He said, 'yeah, you keep on moaning, I'm not changing my position'."

"And what did you say to him?" asked Liam with a sinking feeling.

Con looked him fully in the face, and a reluctant, gleeful smile started to divide his face in two. "Well, I said, 'that's funny, that's exactly what I said to your wife last night'."

Sometimes a victory is not necessary to have a celebration. This team was used to losing, and they took this latest and most painful – defeat as a confirmation of who they were and what they stood for. In great Irish tradition, win or lose, the craic has to go on, and in The Lawless the party went on well into the night. The local gardaí left them to it, knowing well enough when it was time to turn a blind eye. And the sky was brightening again when they all finally fell from the pub and staggered off towards the hired minibus for the journey home.

CHAPTER FIVE

There is nothing like your family for focusing your mind on what is really important in life, and there are few moments in the year as special as Christmas. The parents took it in turns to have other couples' kids round for the day while the mums and dads went off two by two to Castlebar and Ballina for the Christmas shopping. Seán's two would be getting new bikes; Con's eldest needed a new bed, such was the growth spurt he had put on, so Con and Deirdre had decided on a new bedroom more appropriate to his age, complete with his own computer. Cars came back in the dark piled with bags and boxes, and eager children tried their utmost to see what had been bought, and, more importantly, where it was all to be hidden.

There was also the annual club Christmas dinner. Every year there was a different theme – everybody had to come dressed according to the theme, and on top of that all the men had to do something connected to the theme, be it a song, a short sketch or even a striptease involving taking off the fancy dress. The girls were thoughtfully allowed to abstain from making fools of themselves in public, although the rule usually only lasted until the karaoke was turned on.

This year's theme was the mafia, a theme which came round with surprising regularity, and players and partners went to town on dinner jackets and flapper dresses, false Don Corleone moustaches and beauty spots. Inevitably, some of the couples decided to give things a little twist, with the wife coming dressed as Don Corleone and the husband as the moll. There is nothing like a party to give grown men the excuse to force their hairy legs into a pair of tights for the evening.

On the night they piled into the local hotel, greeted the receptionists whose wary smiles already spoke of the evening ahead, and filled a whole dining room with fun. Various players enacted favourite scenes from The Sopranos and Scarface, with those dressed in drag providing enthusiastic female support, while Con and Seán had written their own small play in two scenes about the robbery of a local bank by some particularly bungling masked raiders, with Ger Flynn chosen to play the bank teller and Pádraicín elected to play the part of the unfortunate garda who is equally as bad in his attempts to stop them. However, it was the midfield partnership of Niall O'Byrne and Liam Murphy and left-siders Brian Lynch and Paul O'Connor who stole the show, dressed as gangsters' molls, doing their own – quite faithful – version of 'Bohemian Rhapsody'. The link to the mafia, the second verse, was tenuous at best but nobody cared because the song was an unqualified success and drew the only standing – swaying, by that point – ovation of the night.

In keeping with mafia, there was a casino as well as the usual karaoke as after-dinner entertainment, and again the party continued until the cows wanted milking.

Christmas Day came and family came first again. Con spent breakfast casting thoughtful glances over at a Christmas card that had come from Dublin. Little brother Ciarán was the only one of the family who had left Mayo to go to that other Ireland, the one of lattes and frittatas, the Ireland that seemed to be desperately trying to be England. Finally Con left the card up on the mantelpiece with a quiet smile and tried not to think about the past. The amount of time needed before you can apologise for something comfortably is directly proportionate to how ashamed it made you feel. Sometimes it's years. And Con accepted that everyone who goes away does so until they can come back on their own terms. Time would tell.

At the table, surrounded by his beautiful wife and children, Con was happily immune to thoughts of his last match – or his next one, whoever the opponent would be.

CHAPTER SIX

February

Sunday, February 10th, 2008. National Hurling League Division 2A, first round: Cill Mhantáin 1-16 Maigh Eo 0-17. Ros Comáin 0-11 Cill Dara 2-12.

Division 3, first round: An Longfort 4-19 Sligeach 2-03,

Division 4, first round: Liatroim 0-08 An Cabhán 2-08.

Saturday, February 16th, 2008. National Hurling League Division 2A, round two: Cill Dara 1-15 Maigh Eo 1-14. An Iarmhí 3-19 Ros Comáin 1-13.

THESE GREEN FIELDS

Division three, round two: Tír Eoghain 1-20 Sligeach 3-10.

For four of the Connacht county teams, the season was over already.

CHAPTER SEVEN
March

Ireland blossomed as spring came round. The mild weather heralded the end of the winter, and even though the summer could still be as bad as the previous year, the spring temperatures injected optimism into even the iciest veins. The blue skies and sunshine were reflected in children's faces, and the lushness of the countryside was mirrored in the enthusiasm of its people.

New lambs stood bockety and unsure among the rollercoaster bees and shiny buttercups, and children dawdled along country lanes from the bus stop, soaking in the sunshine with half-closed eyes and freshly-cropped hair. Sandals were even seen in some shops on the main street of Kilbruagh.

Con was fixing up a wall behind the barn when he saw Seán approaching. When Seán had called at the house, Deirdre had given him two cans of lemonade, so when he arrived behind the barn with a cold drink Con was only too willing to set the stones aside for a while and sit in the sun.

They talked about this and that, gossip from around the farms, until Seán dropped the bombshell.

"The other counties have got wind."

"Ah, you're kidding me! That was the last thing we wanted. How did that happen?"

"I've no idea, but obviously somebody spoke out of turn. Maybe somebody that the selectors spoke to, or somebody's secretary, we'll never know."

Con let out a deep breath. "And how did you find out?"

"Well, I've got a cousin back in Sligo, and he rang me there and asked me straight out if it was true that Mayo want to revive the championship. But that's not the worst thing. The worst thing is that he asked me whether that had started with Kilbruagh or not."

"Feck, that's close to the bone. If he'd just heard a rumour about a game against Galway, fair enough, but to know that it came from us is far too accurate for my liking. Especially if the talk is that we want to revive the whole championship. And what did you say?"

"I acted as surprised as I could, but at the revival bit. I said I'd also heard there might be a game against Galway."

"Feck, Seán, what are you going saying that for?"

"Because I wanted to knock down the thing about reviving the championship, Con, I wanted to take the heat out of the whole thing. If he starts talking – and believe me, this particular cousin would talk shite at county level now – then we're up shit creek. We'll get accused of stirring up shite and Galway'll know we want a go at them and then the press'll get involved and the next minute the Croker's ringing. Then the Board will have our bollocks for bangles."

Con stared into the grass and mused over Seán's words. He wasn't wrong. In fact, he hadn't really done anything wrong at all; he had just been trying to put out a fire that somebody else's big gob had started. He crushed the empty can against his thigh almost absent-mindedly. "Fair enough. What do we do now?"

"Well, I reckon the first thing we do is tell Paddy Mac and try and get him to ring Dennehy or Joyce. I really don't fancy doing that bit meself. Do you?"

"Not likely!"

"Then I'll talk to Paddy Mac so, and we'll see if we can't head the shite off somewhere else for now. At least until we're further down the line." He broke off for a moment, deep in thought. "You know, it may not be a bad thing either. It'll give the thing a bit more weight. There'll probably be someone up there in the Croker who'll be grateful we suggested what he couldn't!"

"You reckon? That'll be the day!"

"Sure, why not? That might even be why this got out in the first place, if you know what I mean. Anyway, I've got to be off, I'd better ring Paddy Mac sooner rather than later. See you in the pub later?"

Yeah, see you there. Good luck!"

"What? Ah Seán, how the feck did that happen?"
"What? You want me to talk to them?"
"What? It's my turn for the first round?"

"What? Ah Paddy Mac, I'll have yer bollocks!"
"What? Then I'll have O'Flaherty's bollocks!"

CHAPTER EIGHT

The sun was blinding off the gelid Atlantic water, and Con squinted in pain as he attempted to admire the view from the conservatory of the Connolly ranch. It was a lost cause, so he turned back to face the others, blinking black blotches out of his eyes as he tried to readjust to the slightly more normal light of the interior. He and Seán were waiting on Connolly again, and they were certain they would have to wait even longer than usual so that his grand entrance could outweigh the humiliation of the last meeting.

The two players were surprised when the door opened after only a short time. In came Connolly, accompanied this time by Paddy Mac as well as by Dennehy and Joyce as the lads had anticipated. Their surprise was compounded when they realised that the customary tray of Irish domestic hospitality was borne not by Connolly's daughter but by Ger Lally, head of the Galway county board. He shot the lads an enigmatic smile as he placed the tray carefully on the glass table.

Ger Lally was comparatively young for a selector, having been forced to retire early from playing due to a horrific leg injury from an accident with the tractor. He had bounced back faster than most and had gone straight into club management. Honesty, integrity and a finely-honed ability to sidestep bullshit had helped him to work his way up the county hierarchy, and at forty-two he was the youngest man on the board. He still walked with a limp but talked as straight as the next man.

In spite of the geographical differences – one end of County Mayo to the other end of County Galway – Con had had personal dealings with Ger. When Con was lying in hospital still recovering from his own injuries, Ger had visited him to commiserate about the situation and to wish him well on the road to recovery. He had been brutally honest about Con's chances of playing again, but this honesty, paradoxically, had only encouraged Con in his belief that he could come back.

Anyway, Con had appreciated Ger's gesture and held the man in high regard.

Tea and cake were passed round and the appropriately polite pre-battle noises were made. How's your wife, how's your kids, how's business. When the lull came, Jimmy Dennehy was the first to speak.

"Well gentlemen, thank you all for coming." Nods and muttered replies. "Especially you Ger, I know you're a busy man and we're very grateful for your presence." Respectful murmurs of agreement from the Mayo men. "First of all, I'd like to congratulate you on your appointment to youth development at Croke Park." Barely muffled gasps of astonishment – there was a man from the Croker in the room! – became hurried congratulations. Con and Seán glanced at each other, but stayed quiet. If Dennehy and Joyce had cooked this one up, there would be a very good reason for it.

"Thank you, Jimmy, that's very kind of you. I'd just like to say though," turning now to Paddy Mac and his lads, "that this appointment has absolutely nothing to do with my presence here. I've come because I was invited and because Jimmy said he had something important to discuss, but the new job's a coincidence." *Like Hell,* thought Con, but he kept his thoughts away from his face. "So," continued Ger, "how can I help you?"

Between them, Dennehy, Joyce and Connolly explained about the suggestion to play Galway again, spelled out the potential implications of such a game and assured Ger that this was in no way an attempt to revive the provincial championship. "We just fancy one last game against them, that's all. It would be a fitting send-off for Galway, too, if you think about it."

Ger shifted in his wicker chair and frowned in concentration. "One last game with the neighbours, so. No hard feelings, and all that. Have you mentioned any of this to the others?"

The selectors fell over each other to assure him that Sligo, Leitrim and Roscommon were not involved in any way in the plan. Ger continued frowning as he mulled over the implications in his mind. The other men watched him in expectant silence. Finally he spoke. "Okay so, how would we do this then?"

The selectors and Paddy Mac set about talking through the various aspects of setting up the game. It should be for charity, no it could be a centenary match for the 1909 win, no better that it should be something social with benefits for the wider community. Nothing needs saying to the other counties as it's between Galway and Mayo, no, something should be said to the other counties in case they feel left out.

We need clearance from Croke Park for an inter-county game, no it's a provincial matter, in fact it's just a friendly between representative sides. We need a date, publicity and advertising space, we need to decide on a ground. As they thrashed out the details that Ger would take back to the Galway board, Con and Seán tuned out. Too much politics altogether.

Eventually the peripheral buzzing seemed to slow and the two players focused once more on the conversation. The four selectors and Paddy Mac were all smiling, so it had obviously been a fruitful exchange of views. Now they were on to the stage of praising each other's counties with broad statements of admiration for various aspects of local life.

Con excused himself to go to the bathroom. As he stepped out of the conservatory and closed the door behind him he perceived some movement at the opposite end of the hall, almost as if a door had closed quickly. He walked towards the end of the passageway, his footsteps muffled by the strip of thick, expensive carpet that covered the polished wood and paused a moment before entering the guest bathroom. He was sure there were voices on the other side of the door at the end. Kathleen, maybe, except that they seemed to be men's voices. Whatever, his bladder urged him on. By the time he had returned to the conservatory he had forgotten about it.

The conference had come to an end, and all the participants were on their feet and shaking hands with each other. Smiles all round and it was time to leave. Connolly showed Con, Seán and Paddy Mac out through the door in the conservatory, and Con breathed the Atlantic air in deeply as he savoured the fresh breeze on his face, a welcome change after the humid heat of the conservatory.

He was about to make a comment on the beauty of the view out over the bay when he realised that the other three selectors had not followed them out through the door. As he glanced back over his shoulder he saw them sitting down again in the wicker chairs while Connolly disappeared out of the interior door into the hall. He frowned, but said nothing as they piled into Paddy Mac's battered Carina.

They were out onto the road back towards Kilbruagh when Paddy Mac spoke up.

"What did ye think of that, then lads?" he asked with a wry smile.

For the second time that afternoon Con and Seán exchanged glances, and then they looked at their bainisteoir for enlightenment.

From the silence Paddy Mac realised they were waiting for him to speak, so he glanced at them with a canny look on his face. "Do you not think that was all a bit smooth?

None of our selectors seemed overly put out that the news had been leaked, although I suppose they weren't really going to mention that in front of Ger Lally. But then he accepted the proposal fast enough, with no protest at all and he's convinced he's going to take that back to his Board? And he's just got himself a new job at Croke Park? Seems to me the moment for sitting down and not rocking the boat, lads, what do you say?"

The two players thought about Paddy Mac's words. Sure, it was strange how smoothly everything was going, but then why shouldn't it? It was a fair suggestion, playing Galway again, so the selectors were happy with it. They could do nothing about the leak, so they were not going to get angry about it. Ger Lally was not going to get his feet wet at all, he had simply listened to what they had to say and now he was going to relay the whole conversation to the Galway board. If it came to anything he could just lay the blame for the whole thing firmly at Mayo's door. Just like Seán's cousin in Sligo had. Suddenly, he remembered the closing door and the voices.

"Feck, lads, I think we're being had!"

Now it was the turn of Con and Paddy Mac to share a glance. Con told them of the voices, and then remarked on the fact that the other selectors had sat back down again when the three of them had left.

"You know what I think? When we went to see them the first time, they were quite happy to let bygones be bygones with me. Almost too happy, I thought at the time, you remember Seán, I said as much to you in the car." Seán nodded his agreement and took up the line from where Con had left off.

"And then they were only too happy to listen to our suggestion as well. Sure, they acted surprised for the whole of five seconds then suddenly they were right behind it. Next thing we know they're talking about it back in Sligo. If they know there, they probably know in Leitrim and Roscommon too. Where's Mickey Joyce's wife from again?"

"Sligo," said Paddy Mac with understanding blooming in his voice. "And he gets on grand with her brothers, who are all involved at club level there."

Con continued the conspiracy theory. "So we tell them and they accept it no problem. Then they get Ger Lally in, who's not only Galway he's Croke Park too, and ambitious with it, and we assure him there's no intention of agitating for the championship to be held again. And there were some other fellas in a room at the end of the hall, probably waiting for us to leave."

They were driving over the top of the bog now, and Paddy Mac suddenly pulled over to the gravel at the side of the road. He wrenched up the handbrake and turned to face the two other men.

"Arra shite! Will ye listen to us? What's next, who shot Kennedy? What are we like, jumping to conclusions! You know, at my age I shouldn't be jumping so high, I might hurt something!"

They all laughed, and the laughter relieved the atmosphere that had been building up in the car. They sat and admired the view across the bog to the distant glittering of the Atlantic in silence. Finally Con piped up.

"Fair enough, it's a fairy tale. Mind you, who's to say they don't have their own agenda? Maybe the Board do want the championship brought back. Maybe it's purely a sporting thing, maybe there's cash involved. At the end of the day, that's not our problem. We play a match and walk away. If anyone's going to start pushing for more, it'll be them, and they'll be in the firing line."

"Sure one thing's for certain," interrupted Seán, "if Ger Lally's in on it, Croke Park will know soon enough. And when we hear their reaction, we'll know whether there's going to be bother over it or not."

"And that's when we pack our bags, so?" asked Con. "Flee the country in the dead of night?" He was laughing, and the others smiled too.

"No lads," answered Paddy Mac, "that's when we stand up and be counted. Because I'm telling you, I'm well up for this match now!"

CHAPTER NINE

April

Seán's words proved to be prophetic very soon afterwards. At the start of April Croke Park's press office levered a statement into an article in the Times about the future of the provincial championships. They were eager to demonstrate that they were always ready to listen to the opinions of association members in any county in order to find a way forward which would suit everyone and act in the game's best interests.

In the following days, local newspapers in Sligo, Leitrim and Roscommon carried comments from county board members declaring that they too would always act in the best interests of the game in general, and how better to benefit the game than increasing competition for all counties at all levels?

Of course, all these minor articles and vague comments faded into the background as the counties affected by the Leinster invitation to Galway all made declarations that appeared only to smooth the way for the defection. It seemed that when it eventually came to a vote, there would only be one possible outcome.

All of this was avidly discussed in The Lawless of an evening, although without reaching any significant conclusion. About the only thing they managed to agree on was that it was all politics. Croke Park's response could mean 'yes we'll listen' or 'no, we'll not listen to things that we interpret as not being in the benefit of the game', and possibly 'it is not in the benefit of the game to go backwards down a route already travelled'.

It was also agreed that from the rumblings coming from the rest of Connacht, the other counties might well be interested in a match-up. However, that was as far as the issue could go at that time because nobody knew what Galway would do. Whether they would respond positively or not was anyone's guess, especially as nobody had officially said anything on the subject. Anyway, Galway still had a vested interest in the current season, and with important matches to play in reality they were hardly likely to delve into the realms of fantasy just to please the neighbours.

That apple would take a while to fall from the tree.

PART TWO

CHAPTER TEN

June

Summer truly is the season for Gaelic games. The holidays approach, the weather is stunning, and the flowers that grow in the hedgerows are reflected in the brilliant colours of club and county. Flags fly proudly from pylons and pennants flutter above cars, and the warm-up of the National Leagues gives way to the excitement and spectacle of the All-Ireland qualifiers.

Except that the weather does not always get the message. The mild sunshine and pleasant temperatures of the spring had given way to rain and clouds. Fans and players alike woke up on each match day and poked uncertain faces between curtains with ever-decreasing hope that the match would be played in appropriate summer weather.

Con and Deirdre had worried that this summer would turn out to be the washout that the previous summer had been and had escaped with the kids to Málaga for a week in May in order to at least see some sunshine, and Seán and Ciara had done likewise, escaping to Lanzarote. Now everyone was back in town for the start of another year – the county championship was about to get under way.

Training started in earnest, and all the pints from the close season were run off in intense sessions under Paddy Mac and Seán. Fitness levels improved, and after the previous season's appearance in the provincial final, morale was high. At the back of everybody's mind was a thought that nobody dared voice – would they have the chance of revenge against Kinglen? Or any Galway team, for that matter. With Con especially, the manner of the defeat had left a particularly bad taste in the mouth, and even though time was supposed to heal all wounds, revenge was a decidedly quicker solution.

First, though, they had to get past the best of the county, and by all accounts it would be a difficult year. Confidence was high in more clubs than just Kilbruagh, and in more than one town talented young hurlers had stepped up to the senior team with the promise of delivering many a point over the course of the summer.

For Kilbruagh, the early morale soon took a battering. Rounds one and two were a disaster. Local rivals Patrick Connelly's of Ballyba rode over them in an ill-tempered affair which the enemy won with a fairly comprehensive score of 4-12 to 0-16, before a team from the other side of the county, Belmoy, thrashed them 6-15 to 1-14.

Round three saw the first victory of the year, a close-run affair against a much weaker side that everybody would beat over the five rounds, but as the leaders sailed away into the distance the confidence in the Kilbruagh camp and the expectations of the start of the summer all but dissipated under a cloud of depression.

CHAPTER ELEVEN

Saturday, June 28th, 2008. All-Ireland Senior Hurling Championship, qualifiers: Aontroim 1-10 Gaillimh 6-21.

Galway steamroller their way over Antrim and march on, apparently fearing nobody.

CHAPTER TWELVE

July

Pádraicín leaned back against the stone wall and closed his eyes to the early morning sunshine. This was the best time of day for him, early morning peace and quiet combining with what usually turned out to be the best weather of the day too.

In his hands he clutched his breakfast roll, his bottle of Lucozade and the folded-up newspaper. The same breakfast as every day of his working life, with very little variation. He smiled in the sunshine and waited patiently for Niall to appear in the van to take them both to the site. Thirty new exclusively private luxury homes built with you in mind. Whatever, it was a wage and food on the table. He was a dab hand with the bricks and mortar but it was no love affair, it was just a job that paid the rent. He lived for the hurling and the craic in the pub afterwards.

Niall arrived on time in his used-to-be-white van, paused momentarily to let his friend up into the passenger seat and then tore away round the country lanes. Pádraicín stored his breakfast on the dashboard as he always did, and struggled with his seat belt. It eventually clicked, and he settled back to read the day's headlines out to Niall.

The driver of the powerful BMW was so short he could barely see above the steering wheel, and to compound the fact he insisted on sitting low in the seat because that was the cool way to do it. Of course, he considered himself to be a good driver, and he was proud of the fact that he did not drink and drive any more; he had left that behind in his twenties. He always drove fast because it was a fast car and that was what fast cars were for, and anyway, he had not spent all that money on the car just to drive it like his dad. And he could handle the speed; it was the other drivers who needed to learn how to deal with the road conditions, not him. Obviously he was right, because so far he had never had a crash.

As Niall came round the corner, hugging the hedge so much he could hear the brambles scraping along the side, he encountered the other car in the middle of the road. Even though it had a good three feet of clearance it made no attempt to move over or even slow down, it just flashed its lights in annoyance. Niall tried braking but it was too late; the speed of the BMW made the accident inevitable.

The impact destroyed the car; the van flipped up and was thrown into the field, coming to a rest on its roof. The explosion of noise caused by the accident cleared away into a tense silence, which faded into nothing as the birds took up where they had left off. At the far side of the field, a herd of cows watched impassively for a few moments, but as nothing else moved they continued chewing the lush grass.

Twenty minutes later an old farmer, expecting to find a tractor round every corner and therefore travelling the country roads at a much more modest speed, came round the corner and braked just in time to avoid hitting the smoking pile of metal that used to be the BMW. He stared at the wreckage for a second, as if he expected it to be a trick of his old eyes, then he gingerly reversed back round the corner a little so that his car was visible to any traffic coming in the same direction. There had been nobody behind him, but just in case. He flicked on the hazards and called the gards.

The local gards were prompt and efficient. They closed the road at two different junctions and inspected the vehicles. The driver of the BMW was woven into the mangled wreckage. Pádraicín was unresponsive, Niall barely breathing. An ambulance and a fire engine arrived minutes after the gards and set about removing the three people from the wrecked vehicles.

It wasn't long before other people from the area gathered at the barriers set up by the gards, and the talk started as to who it was, how the accident had happened and how awful it was that nothing was being done about reckless driving habits. A local journalist listened in discreetly before pulling his camera from his bag and edging along the hedge on the field side. When he reached the wreckage of the van he took a few shots before leaning through the brambles to see what was left of the car.

He had his own set of rules for road traffic accidents – get the wreckage and any bodies, covered or otherwise, then get a shot with some blood and something personal. There should always be an item of clothing, or maybe a bag if the victim was a woman, but clothes were better. Especially if there were children involved, a child's shoe in the middle of the road was perfect for giving the shot that human angle that would touch everyone's feelings. It was the next best thing to getting an actual body, something at which most editors would balk.

THESE GREEN FIELDS

There was a puddle of oil in the middle of the road, close to the wrecked BMW. Click click. In the newspaper, in black and white, it could look like blood. No shoe, no problem. He always carried one around with him for situations just like these. He pulled it out of his bag, checked that the gards still had not seen him there and pitched the shoe into the middle of the road. Click click.

A flurry of phone calls followed during the day as the local channels of communication buzzed live with the news. Soon everybody in the area had a more or less accurate version of events, leaving out the more far-fetched details of the gossips of our sensationalist imaginations. The families of Pádraicín and Niall were informed of the accident by the local gardaí and were rushed to the county hospital in a state of shocked silence.

Con arrived with Ger Flynn just before lunchtime, and found Niall's wife and sister and Pádraicín's brother slumped in plastic chairs in the waiting area. Sympathetic nurses were keeping them informed, but as yet there was very little information to give. The five of them shared disjointed comments in hushed tones as Con tried hard to ignore the smell of disinfectant and the atmosphere of urgent hopelessness of the intensive care unit.

Shortly after twelve a nurse came out with that look on her face that every family dreads. *I'm very sorry Mister Kavanagh. We did everything we could.* Pádraicín's brother collapsed back in the chair fighting back the tears. Niall's sister put an arm round his enormous shoulders while looking up at the nurse with fear etched across her face. *Mister O'Byrne is critical but stable. We're keeping him under constant observation and we'll let you know as soon as his conditions changes.* Relief for Niall's wife and sister; a stay of execution.

As the afternoon wore on other club members came and went, expressed their support to Niall's family and spoke with quiet regret in discreet corner conversations. Shock and condemnation had given way to prayers of hope that at least Niall would pull through. Con had taken Pádraicín's brother home; as his only family, the brother had no-one to tell. All he had left to do was to bury his brother next to his parents and live the rest of his life on his own.

That evening the players gathered in The Lawless and quietly nursed their pints around the tables. Conversation was limited to grunted sentences as the men drowned their loss in their beer. Close to closing time Con's phone rang. He peered at the phone a moment as if afraid of it and then grabbed it and jumped nervously to his feet. He held a brief monosyllabic conversation and then hung up with a plastic snap.

"That was Paddy Mac."

"Christ, is he still at the hospital?"

"Shush, yes, now listen to Con."

"He said Niall's out of danger now apparently. They had to operate on him, on his chest, but they reckon he's much better now than when he came in. He's still under and everything, but they reckon he'll wake up."

The news was greeted with sighs of relief and nervous smiles from the players. Seán jumped up and ordered another round from Jackie as the players sat up a little straighter around the small pub tables.

Everyone knew Pádraicín and the entire area turned out for the funeral, filling the small local church to accompany him in his final journey. Father Dónal grew in stature for the occasion, the tiny priest speaking eloquently about friendship and loss and community.

After the service the black procession threaded its way round the winding lanes to the local cemetery, where a few more words were said over Pádraicín before he was laid to rest. The crowd lingered among the sun-drenched graves and told stories of their friend's escapades and mishaps until laughter beat the tears.

CHAPTER THIRTEEN

The day after the funeral, Con was back working behind the barn, attempting to cut back the dogwood. It was a rare day of sunshine, although the sky was starting to threaten to throw a hissy fit before the afternoon was out. He heard a car pull up in front of the house, and imagined it must be the postman. He continued pruning the sturdy red branches. The engine died and did not start up again. Con strained to filter something from the silence.

He was about to go round the barn to the house to see who the visitor was when he was brought up short by the sound of footsteps. Not the steady, heavy footsteps of a person accustomed to trudging round farms, but the fussy syncopated walk of the city-dweller. He waited for a moment, watching the corner of the barn, and was astonished when the visitor finally showed himself.

The man was smaller than Con, slimmer too and less athletic, and he was dressed in a nice striped shirt and a stylish sweater. However, in spite of the differences in physique and fashion there was a determination about the set of the jaw and a rugged defiance in the eyes that marked him out as an O'Coolahan. The prodigal brother had come home to roost.

He picked his way across the uneven ground, not daring to look up in case he fell, and he had already almost arrived to where Con was standing before he realised there was someone watching him. He stopped suddenly and looked up, swaying slightly as he tried to keep his shiny shoes on the summit of a mossy rock.

"Hi Con."

Con stood stock still, the giant secateurs hanging from one hand.

"Ciarán."

"How you doing?"

"Grand, and yourself?"

"Well enough."

"Is Deirdre in the house?"

"She is." Ciarán tried to gesture back towards the house but the effort nearly toppled him from his mossy perch. He swayed again, and decided to stand as still as his brother.

"Then you get yourself back to the house and get a cup of tea, and I'll be in when I'm finished out here, okay?"

Ciarán considered this for a moment, and appearing to decide that it was a reasonable offer, smiled and turned gingerly to retrace his cautious steps back round the barn and out of sight.

Con continued chopping at the dogwood, but stopped after a few moments because it was far too dangerous to carry on this activity when his mind was somewhere completely different. He straightened up and absent-mindedly clipped the secateurs shut, gazing out across the stone wall into the distant fields. Somewhere over there was the bay, and the beach he always ran along, and right now he would have given anything to be out there and running, instead of stuck here with the past staring him in the face. He was tired of having to sort things out, but he had the grace to admit, if only to himself, that he would not have to sort so much out if he could control his temper.

And then he remembered. Ciarán had been Pádraicín's best friend at school. Con mentally chided himself for being so self-centred. Ciarán had heard about Pádraicín and had come home to pay his respects. He would be upset, and the last thing he would need was another row.

He sighed and set off for the house.

Deirdre and Ciarán were sat at the kitchen table chatting comfortably. Deirdre had always got on well with both of Con's brothers, which in the case of Ciarán had annoyed Con intensely. He felt that his wife should always take his side in any dispute, at least in public, whether he was right or wrong. Deirdre agreed with this to a certain extent – she would always back her husband up in public in order to present a united front even if she meant to tear strips off him in private for being an idiot – but in her book there was no 'private' or 'public' when it came to family. Family was always private in the face of the rest of the world, but it was always public within. So when Con and Ciarán had rowed, and Ciarán had left for Dublin, Deirdre had slated Con for his attitude.

Although he would never admit it, Con was shaken when he stepped through the kitchen door and found his wife and his brother sitting there as if nothing had happened. The last row had taken place while they were first sitting, then standing round this very table. Standing, fists clenched, spitting out words that could only hurt, that had to hurt because that was the only way each man could score a victory. Deirdre had tried to intervene up to a point, the point at which she could see that both brothers had lost all sense of dignity and proportion and would continue fighting until they had torn their relationship definitively apart. Then she had sat down and cried, out of frustration and fear that they had gone to a place from which they could never or would never return.

Con sat down at the table and looked at his brother. The six years in Dublin had been kind to him. He looked tanned and well-dressed, and Con knew he would be accepted in circles that he could never access. In spite of their rows he was still proud of his little brother and what he was capable of achieving. He looked down at his own hands, and saw them suddenly in a different light, as thick sausages with dirty broken nails. In his mind he equated his nails and his brothers' suits to their different outlooks on life. Con the dirty fighter, Ciarán the polished negotiator.

Con would never know this, but at that very same moment his brother was comparing the two of them as well, and saw in Con's strong hands the honesty of the land and the courage of those who stay and fight. His own suits now just spoke to him of flight and falsehood. However, neither brother voiced his thoughts. The truth is often far more difficult to say than an insult.

Deirdre poured Con a cup of tea, and Con looked up again, coming back to the conscious reality of the kitchen. He smiled his thanks at his wife for the tea, and took the plunge.

"I'm really sorry about Pádraicín, Ciarán; I know you were close at school."

"Thanks, Con, same to you. I know you were close on the team as well."

Deirdre breathed more easily through the uneasy silence. That was a good start. They sipped their tea and tried to drag topics of conversation into blank minds, discarding many a sentence for fear it might be taken the wrong way. Finally Con broke the silence again.

"I'll take you up to the grave later. Take you round to his brother's, if you want. He'd be pleased to see you."

"Yeah, grand, we can do that."

"You staying long?"

"I might, if that's alright?" A glance at Deirdre, who waved any doubt away.

"You on holiday so?" asked Con

"No. I've left the job. I was tired of it. Packed it in."

Con let the surprise show on his face. "Wow. I thought you really liked it there? In that firm, I mean."

"Well, I always swore I'd never come back home, but only ever in moments when I knew I didn't have to!"

"Don't worry, I still swear I'll never become office fodder, and I will until the day I'm out of work! But seriously, that firm was okay, wasn't it?"

"It was, but I was getting tired of working for someone else. I'm qualified now, so I can be an accountant for myself." A pause. "And anywhere I want, too." Another pause. "I was thinking of coming back home and trying my luck here, Castlebar maybe, or Ballina. I reckon there's a fair few farmers need their affairs putting in order. I might try setting myself up in that way, you know, providing a service for the local community. At a cost, of course," he finished with a smile.

Con laughed, secretly delighted at the news. "Aye, well, you'll earn your fees if you can make some of this lot round here part with their cash, that's for sure!"

"That's grand, Ciarán, and you can stay here as long as you like, you know that," said Deirdre, taking her brother-in-law's hand. "You're always welcome here."

Con gulped down the rest of his tea, worried that the conversation might take a turn for the teary. "Come on, I'll drive you down to Pádraicín now. Or better still, you can chauffeur me round in that fancy thing of yours. It's about time I started reaping the fruits of my labours."

"What labours, brother?" asked Ciarán with a wicked smile.

"The labours of teaching a little brother everything he knows!"

CHAPTER FOURTEEN

Round four of the T.J. Tyrell Cup saw Kilbruagh at home to a team from up beyond, Naomh Pádraig. The match was to be played the weekend after Pádraicín's funeral, and the hundreds of local people who had packed out the church and spilled out among the old stone graves now stood around the painted wooden fencing as a further gesture of support to the dead goalkeeper's brother.

In a huge national stadium there would be banners, pictures of the player on giant screens, eloquent tributes from the commentators. This was the back of beyond, and things were much simpler. This was the place where people buried their dead in the small local cemetery and walked past them every day, where farmers lost animals and moved on to the next job, where families still held vigils so that the entire population of the townland could file past and have a last look. They were much closer to death here, and accepted it as being as much a part of life as being born.

The team stood in a long line along the sixty-five, their arms wrapped round each other's shoulders and a narrow strip of black gaffer tape around their sleeves. The Naomh Pádraig players stood in respectful silence on their own sixty-five. The referee and linesmen walked to the middle of the pitch and stood with their hands behind their backs and their heads bowed, signalling the start of a minute's silence.

Nobody was sure who started it off, but a ripple of applause broke out among the supporters along the fencing. The staccato noise grew in confidence and reached a crescendo as the two teams, surprised at the spontaneous outburst of affection but understanding it nevertheless, joined in. The applause lasted for a full minute until the referee let out a sharp blast on his whistle. The applause turned to cheering. Game on.

The Kilbruagh team played with a passion born of their loss, but the Naomh Pádraig players had failed to read the script. They were sorry for their opponents' loss; every community knows the pain of losing one of its own too young, but they had come to win, and win they did. At the end of the game, Seán's men trudged off disconsolately. They had wanted to send Pádraicín off with a victory and they had failed him. In the dressing room, the tears that they had choked back at the funeral came out in a flood.

THESE GREEN FIELDS

CHAPTER FIFTEEN

Saturday, July 5th, 2008. All-Ireland Senior Hurling Championship, qualifiers: Gaillimh 1-26 Laoise 0-9.

Sunday, 13th July, 2008. Connacht Senior Football Championship Final, McHale: Gaillimh 2-12 Maigh Eo 1-14.

Galway's senior football side come up to Mayo, pillage the provincial trophy and march back home with their heads – and the trophy – held high.

Saturday, July 19th, 2008. All-Ireland Senior Hurling Championship, qualifiers: Gaillimh 2-15 Corcaigh 0-23.

Galway's hurlers are finally stopped in their tracks by a superior Rebel side. The next time they will play an official match, in the National League, it will be as a Leinster team.

CHAPTER SIXTEEN

August

Round five, and Kilbruagh were obliged to travel down the N59, across Achill Sound and out to the far side of Achill Island to meet the warriors of Tragagh. Everybody hated coming out here to play, not least because of the name of the area. Nobody really knew the origin of the word, but it was too close to '*tréigthe*' for comfort. And it really did look abandoned.

Ireland is like any other country in that its geography has the personality of its people stamped all over it. There are posh counties where the countryside is excessively polite, contrived even, while under the neat exterior it is still dirt.

Then there are places where the land is more natural, wilder, untouched since a more primitive time, with interesting things hidden away.

As the bus drove the last couple of miles to the GAA ground, the players knew which part of Ireland they were in. This was real countryside, with centuries-old stone walls to protect it, and none of this wooden fence nonsense. The only sign of life was three horses gossiping over a wall. The team knew from the wild, rocky surroundings that they were here to have their bodies battered and their spirit crushed.

There was no settlement, simply a collection of farms scattered far enough away from the next one for the neighbours never to see each other, let alone annoy each other. High on a cliff overlooking the doom of the Atlantic was an old chapel, just below it a cemetery, and below that a rough patch of ground with posts at either end. The dressing rooms were the bit of grass on the discreet side of the bus, and the nets on the posts were old fishing nets. The pitch was uneven and rocky; the Tragagh team was unstable and stony.

Tragagh bet Kilbruagh off the pitch, physically, mentally and every other way. Con and Ger were so put off by the naked aggression of their opponents that their shooting was a danger to shipping, and even the normally reliable Liam Murphy could not hit a cow's arse with the proverbial banjo.

THESE GREEN FIELDS

When the referee blew for an infringement close to the end of the match, the Kilbruagh team decided to pretend that they had heard the final whistle and as one trooped off the field simply to escape the battering. They drove back home in subdued mood, comparing wounds and drinking cans of beer in morose silence.

Their short official season was over, and it was a season they were desperate to forget.

CHAPTER SEVENTEEN
September

It is the first Sunday in September and Croke Park is packed with people and bright with colour as Kilkenny thrash Waterford 3-30 to 1-13 to complete three All-Irelands in a row.

Before the big game throws in, Ger Lally meets suits and ties from the other four Connacht counties and tells them, in the privacy of a store-room, that if they want a fight he will meet them outside after the game. Figuratively speaking, of course.

PART THREE

CHAPTER EIGHTEEN
October

It is surprising how quickly and how quietly the relevant decisions were made by the people that mattered, especially considering, under normal circumstances, how many meetings had to be chaired and how many layers of bureaucracy had to be penetrated before even the smallest changes could be countenanced. When you have the members of over 1,600 clubs to please, it is obviously a slow process.

In this case, however, it was decided that if the Connacht counties wanted to have it out in their own back yard, without affecting anybody else in the country, and without impinging on any other inter-county competitions, well then, they could do as they pleased. To have a small, discreet run-out in the winter could be said to be beneficial to all the counties concerned if the games were considered to be merely challenge matches played as preparation for the coming season.

It's a local thing, that's all it is.

It is astonishing how a small local affair can be blown so brutally out of proportion, especially considering that the county boards simply had to organise a couple of matches. When the blood of the ancients is at stake, it is obviously going to be a bloody process.

The first argument was over the structure of the competition. Galway – in their opinion, quite reasonably – suggested that as they were reigning champions of Connacht and quite obviously the best team, the other four counties should play two semi-finals and then a final to decide who should have the privilege of challenging Galway for whatever little tin pot they wanted to play for.

The response was almost Mediterranean in its intensity. Hands were thrown in the air and eyes rolled round and strong words were spoken. In Sligo they declared that as it was a one-off competition the five counties should start as equals and their names be put into a pot in order to draw for qualifiers. In the age-old tradition of complicating GAA qualification beyond all logic or understanding, one team would receive a bye in the first round and another would receive one in the second (and effectively reach the final after winning just one game).

Eyebrows were raised in Leitrim at the backwardness of their neighbours, and it was proposed that in the interests of fairness there should be at least two games each so that everybody had a decent chance of progressing. In fact, why not hold a round-robin competition?

Roscommon laughed up their sleeves at their poor, deluded neighbours and declared that if a knock-out structure was enough for other provincial championships – careful, there – then it would be fine for them too, blind to the fact that they were suggesting something similar to both Galway and Sligo.

And in Mayo they stood watching, scratching their heads at how a simple observation by a child had turned into war.

Of course, the situation would not have descended into farce so easily if they all knew what they were fighting for. In spite of Croke Park's insistence that it would be an insignificant local spat there was a growing feeling among the counties concerned that it was something much more serious than that. The situation came to a head when Sligo, Leitrim and Roscommon declared that in order to bring Galway down the necessary peg or two it had to be a provincial championship or nothing. Mayo again wandered round on the periphery, provoking the ire of all four rivals who made it clear they viewed such fence-sitting with the utmost disdain.

Galway's response to the apparent aggression was to declare that it could indeed be a provincial championship, but that Croke Park would have to decide on the format. Croke Park said that under no circumstances would they back down on their previous decision and that any county defying their instructions – that it was no more than a local affair and certainly not a revival of the provincial championship – would be declared in rebellion. Unfortunately for Croke Park it was a slow news month in the west. 'Rebel! Rebel!' screamed the headlines of every newspaper in Connacht, urging the People to rise up against the Dictatorship. Croke Park had a headache already, so they again told the counties to do whatever the feck they wanted. Oh, but Galway are the reigning champions, so they're in charge.

The Galway board rubbed its hands in glee and declared that the others could fight among themselves and they would wait for the winners. They would be waiting in Carraroe, where Galway United had famously dragged a scared Dutch soccer team to be dealt with in the darkest years of the eighties. And in a fit of pettiness, they said they would only be waiting until the end of November, so that if by some miracle Mayo won, they could not say it was a hundred years.

Beware the anger of a patient county board.

CHAPTER NINETEEN
November

Con and Seán were out shopping in Ballina, trying to impress their wives yet again with the best possible Christmas presents. Every year they found themselves caught out on Christmas Eve, searching the local shops for something special that not only would their wives love but that they had not already seen and dismissed as either too expensive or not the right colour. This year they had made a pact to set aside one Saturday – well before the Christmas panic started – to find just one decent present for each wife.

Like any good soldiers faced with a difficult mission they had decided on a plan of action. They would set off early and get over there in time for the shops to open. They would do the lingerie ones first so as not to have to contend with the embarrassment of having to face any other girls apart from the ones working in the shops, who would hopefully be far too asleep to even care at that time of the morning. Then they would try other clothes shops before they got packed with the usual Saturday morning crowd, before moving on to bookshops, and as a last resort, jewellers.

The plan started to go wrong before they had even reached Ballina. They were sat in a small roadside place halfway between their beds and their destiny, sipping scalding coffee and munching on pastries; they needed all the energy they could get. Con was going over some of the details again.

"Did you check herself's sizes?" Seán instantly looked highly embarrassed and buried his face in his pastry. "Oh man, you mean you don't know what her sizes are?"

Seán looked down at both hands and then thought better of it. He swallowed and started to stutter.

"Spit it out lad! Not the pastry!"

"Con, I swear I gave it my best shot, but I just couldn't bring myself to go through her underwear looking at labels. I was so scared of getting caught. And I couldn't trust myself to leave everything as I had found it and I was worried that she'd catch me that way." The words were flowing well enough now. "You know, it's that thing about going through a woman's underwear. She'd think I was a pervert or something."

Con was in stitches. "Seán, you're her husband. You're the father to her children. You're not some spotty teenager trying to sneak a look at his sister's friend's knickers, man." Seán blushed even deeper and Con roared with laughter. "Oh God, I don't want to know! Actually, yes I do!"

The silence and Con's delighted stare had the desired effect on Seán. "No, you see, it wasn't quite like that. We were all round at me cousin's, you remember me cousin Aisling, well my sister Gráinne and me cousin Aisling were in Aisling's room, and their friend Mary was in there with them. Oh God, did I have a thing about Mary. I was thirteen, she was fifteen like Gráinne, and she was stunning. Jet black hair and black eyes that cut through you. She seemed to know what I was thinking just by looking at me, no, she did know what I was thinking. It didn't take a fecking genius to know what went through my mind every time I saw her. Anyway, she scared the living bejaysus out of me, so every time I saw her I froze and started babbling like an eejit. So there they all were, in me cousin Aisling's room, trying on clothes for some birthday party they had."

"Oh Christ, I can see where this is going!"

"Oh yes. And I was stuck in the kitchen, bored out of me tree listening to my ma, me aunt and Mary's ma going about on about the neighbours. There wasn't even a telly. So we'd been there all afternoon when me ma said, 'Seán, go and find your sister cos it's time to go'. So off I went, but I didn't realise that Mary's ma had come out of the kitchen behind me to fetch her girl too. So off up the stairs I go, and I get to the door, but just as I'm about to knock I tripped on the carpet – don't ask me how – and fell against the door and it burst open. So there's Mary, stood there in her knickers and bra, and me sister Gráinne and me cousin half naked as well I think, although believe me I only had eyes for Mary. Anyway, I froze as I always did and just stared at her, and she just stared back, and to this day I swear she had the slightest smile on those luscious lips of hers. It was like she was enjoying me watching her."

"Enjoying playing with you, don't you mean? Fecking with yer head?"

"Oh God. But anyway, as I'd burst in, obviously the other two started screaming and Mary's mother came storming up the stairs behind me and found me staring at her daughter stood there in her knickers. I could hear more footsteps too and suddenly I realised the huge amount of shite that was gathering above me and was about to rain down. I looked round in panic just as Mary's ma reached me, and she grabbed me by the arm and she said, 'what's this, Seány, you sneaking a look at my girl in her knickers, were you?' Well, I shat meself. Me ma and me aunt arrived at the top of the stairs too, and I was surrounded by six women, all holding up my shame for a good look. I would never live it down." He paused for a sip of coffee.

"So how did you get out of it, because three kids tells me you've still got your balls?"

"I just started blabbering out this protest, 'no, Missus Feeney, I swear' and d'you know what she said to me?"

"Go on!"

"She smiled the most evil smile I've ever seen on the face of a human being, and she said, 'what, Seány, are you saying my girl's not good enough for you?' Christ, it was the worst moment of me life, I can tell you. I started trying to protest the opposite and the bedroom door slammed shut and behind the door it was all howls and screams, you know that way girls squeal when some lad's made a total eejit of himself in public, but the worst thing of all was the way the three mothers all laughed. Ah Con, I swear to you I wanted the carpet to swallow me up. Then of course we had it in the car all the way home, and again over tea when me da got in, and then in school on the Monday morning cos they'd told everyone at

124

the birthday party. Feck, I thought my life had come to an end."

"Christ, Seán, what a story, man! Have you ever told herself about this?"

"Don't. When I met Ciara you remember she was working in that shop in Westport in the holidays? Well that shop belonged to Mary's uncle Tomás, and one day I saw Mary coming out of there. I had to do that thing where you suddenly change direction on the pavement, I nearly killed this auld one behind me, and I had to duck into the local pub until I was sure she had gone. From then on it was the longest summer of my life. So no, I never told her. And no, I didn't go through her knickers either."

"Fair enough lad, I'll let you off this time. With your track record, I think we'll steer well clear of the lingerie, what do you think?"

"Yeah, I reckon that'd be a good idea. Let's just go straight to music and books, eh, just to be on the safe side."

The two lads were in the queue for the till when Seán's phone bleeped to tell him he had a text message. He read the message and leaned in to speak over Con's shoulder.

"Galway have changed their mind about the stadium. It'll be at Pearse after all. Must have thought twice about the crowds."

As Con was turning to reply, his phone bleeped with a text message too. He pulled out his phone, read the message and turned to nudge Seán.

"See this. They've just done the draw. We've got Roscommon, away. Sligo and Leitrim in Sligo. Next Saturday. Game on, boy!"

CHAPTER TWENTY

The following week passed in a whirlwind for the Mayo players. In spite of their poor showing in the Tyrell, Kilbruagh had five players called up to the panel – Con, Seán, Ger Flynn at centre forward, Liam Murphy at midfield and Paul O'Connor at left half-back – and they spent the week in extra training for the game. They had no doubts that they would beat Roscommon, but they could not afford to fall at the first hurdle, especially as everybody was blaming them for the whole affair anyway.

Friends and neighbours wished them well, and some local companies even put up the roadside banners normally reserved for the All-Ireland. A couple of journalists from Mayo newspapers rang them up in the evening for quotes ahead of the game, and by the time Friday evening came the players were more psyched up by the hype that was growing up around them than by their own nerves.

Saturday morning finally came, and the players gathered outside McHale Park for the bus ride across to Roscommon town. They would be playing the match at Doctor Hyde Park; the Roscommon board wanted as much support as possible, and although the game probably would not attract the 30,000 capacity, there was a fair amount of interest.

The two games would be played simultaneously, and modern technology meant that in each stadium they would know instantly what was happening in the other. It did not really matter who was winning the other game or who the victors would meet in the next game; it was the 'ooh' factor, nothing more.

The stadium was three-quarters full and the crowd was in good voice as the teams strode out into the bright November sunshine. The referee wasted no time in throwing in, and Mayo wasted no time in pulling away on the scoreboard with four points in the first ten minutes. From then on Roscommon were always chasing the game, and by half-time the lead was almost unassailable. There would need to be a miracle in the second half for Roscommon to catch up.

In the dressing room at half time, the Mayo players were relaxed and confident. At this rate they could easily reach the final against Galway, and possibly even give them a run for their money.

"Calm down, lads," said Ger Nolan, the Mayo bainisteoir, "we've not even won this one yet. And who are we playing next, is there any news yet?"

One of the lads checked the text messages on his phone. "Looks like it could be Sligo, they're up by a goal and three points. If it stays that way it's us and Sligo."

The second half produced no surprises in either game. Mayo continued to pulverise the poor Roscommon team, and Sligo refused to relinquish their lead over Leitrim. Ger Flynn bagged himself a hat trick of goals and a round of applause from the generous Roscommon fans at the final whistle.

Tuesday evening training at Kilbruagh, and the players were chatting about the match against Sligo the following weekend. As always there were different opinions as to the strengths and weaknesses of the opposition side, but they were all agreed that they could beat them, if not as easily as they had beaten Roscommon, then still with some room to spare.

After the training session, there was going to be a pub quiz in The Lawless, with the proceeds going towards the rebuilding of the club bar. Local builders had pledged some pro-bono help – bits and pieces from other jobs that some other client had already paid for – but they had stated they wanted to see some money on the table first.

The players piled into the pub to find their wives and family already in full flow. They gathered in small teams round the tables and cracked jokes as Jackie Lawless passed answer sheets and pencils round the tables. His wife was in as extra help to put pints on the tables as quickly as possible.

Before they started Paddy Mac stood up.

"Well now, it's great to see such a good turnout for the biggest charity case this county has seen since Liam turned up." Laughter round the tables. "We've been talking in the club, and it has been decided that we should give the new building a name and we can vote on it if necessary. So what I was thinking was, if each team takes an answer sheet and writes a suitable name on the back, and then we'll read the names out and vote on them, alright?"

There was more laughter and considerable whispering as the teams' heads went together to discuss a suitable name, followed by intense scribbling and scratching of lead and paper.

"Paddy, how do you spell 'shebeen'?"

"Paddy, how do you spell 'the'?"

"How do you spell 'intoxication'?"

"Who's that with the big words, then?"

After a few minutes all the teams had decided, and amid more drinking jokes Jackie went round and picked up all the folded pieces of paper. He passed them to Paddy Mac at the bar and went to prepare his question sheets. Paddy Mac unfolded the pieces of paper one by one, and the smile slowly disappeared from his face. When he reached the last piece of paper he blinked a couple of times before speaking.

"Well ladies and gentlemen. How do you spell 'unanimous'? It looks like ye're all agreed that the new building will be called 'The Pádraig Kavanagh Clubhouse' and the bar will go by the name of 'Pádraicín's'. I think we'll say that's carried."

A huge cheer went up from the players, who were delighted that they were on an identical wavelength. Paddy Mac sat down at one of the tables, discreetly wiping his eyes on a sleeve, and Jackie stepped up with an old silver microphone. When he had managed to get everyone's attention with the dodgy sound system, the quiz was under way.

THESE GREEN FIELDS

Another Saturday, another game, except on this occasion it was the last qualifier to play Galway in the final. This time the players who gathered outside McHale Park did not need to get on a bus, because they had already arrived at their destination. They piled into the dressing room, laughing and pushing each other. Confidence was as high as it could be after the previous week's result, and when they heard the Sligo players moving around in the away dressing room they increased the noise levels to let their opponents know who should be scared.

Out on the pitch it was a perfect day, bright and sunny but cool enough to be running around for seventy minutes. The referee threw in and the battle commenced. Sligo had obviously come with the intention of taking the game to Mayo, and they hustled and pushed for the first fifteen minutes, limiting Mayo to a single point in reply to Sligo's five. After the initial pressure though they backed off and slowed their pace, which allowed Mayo to come back into the game more strongly. In a ten-minute period in the middle of the half Mayo pulled the score back to within a point. Then disaster struck. With five minutes to go to half time, Sligo slipped through the Mayo defence and slotted a goal into the bottom corner of the goal. It was a heavy psychological blow, and the teams would go in at half time with very different levels of confidence with which to face the rest of the game.

There were stern words at half time in the Mayo dressing room, especially for the defence. They were well aware that the minutes before half time were a crucial time to be alert in defence, because a goal or even just a couple of well-taken points would go without reply and give the scoring side the edge coming back out. The bainisteoir called for concentration, and the skipper yelled some more.

However, the simplest words, from Seán, had the most effect.

"Do you fellas not want a pop at Galway then?"

Mayo came out raging in the second half and immediately set about the task of clawing the points back. Sligo had anticipated the onslaught and held on bravely, and for nearly twenty minutes it looked like they might be able to maintain the lead they had built up in the first half. But Mayo were not a team to be made nervous by ticking clocks, and little by little they dragged their way back to a point's difference.

With less than ten minutes to go a free found its way into the Sligo square. The slíotar bounced awkwardly on a divot and the keeper, wrong-footed, could only flick it out into the path of an onrushing Ger Flynn, who pelted it back across the keeper and into the bottom corner. Another free sailed over the posts and Sligo needed a goal to stay in it. It was Mayo's turn to defend their lead, but instead they drove the advantage home with another two points to seal the victory. Sligo had fought well, but finished on their knees. A relieved Mayo team, worthy winners in the end, would face Galway for the title.

CHAPTER TWENTY-ONE

Con and Deirdre were asleep already; they were always early to bed and early to rise, although the healthy, wealthy and wise bit seemed always to escape Con. He was dreaming he was being chased through the woods behind the house by the cows, and they were gaining on him. He could feel the panic of the prey and he knew he would be caught.

Through the trees he could see a light. What was it? A house? A fire? Whatever, it could be his salvation, so he pressed on through the curtains of dense midnight blackness. At the same time he could feel a force pulling him upwards, towards the surface of something intangible, towards the surface of sleep.

He became conscious of the flashing light of his mobile phone almost before his eyes had had the chance to open. He blinked in the harsh aquamarine light and tried to focus his attentions on reality. He was in bed, asleep. No, awake. Someone was trying to ring him. He wanted to ignore it, but it could be something serious. Long gone were the days of night-time pranks; a call at this time of night did not bode well.

He lay still for a second, monitoring his wife's deep breathing. She was well gone and would not be aware of the call. Better to keep it that way until he knew what was happening. He reached out for the phone, which had stopped flashing and started again, and tried to focus his eyes on the screen without being blinded. Seán. He had better answer it.

"Seán, wait a second," he whispered into the phone as he flipped it open, simultaneously trying to crawl out of bed. It was impossible with one hand attached to the side of his head, so he closed the phone and rolled out of his bed. He padded across the darkened floor and crept out into the hall. He pressed the speed dial button for Seán, needing a couple of attempts before he was successful.

"Seán, what's the craic man, it's past midnight? You what? You're going where? You're outside now with who, have ye gone fecking mad, Seán? Alright, five minutes. I don't care if it is fecking cold, what time do you call this to be out?"

He slipped back into the room and grabbed some clothes. He generally did not worry about style, so at this time of the night he wouldn't either. Just as long as he had his own jeans and not Deirdre's, he would be grand.

He dressed in the kitchen and eased himself out of the kitchen door into the yard. Liam Murphy's work van was sat there with the headlights dimmed. Liam flashed the headlights, unnecessarily Con thought as he stopped to blink the sharp pain out of his head, and opened the passenger door for Con.

Con climbed in and blinked round at the motley crew assembled before him: Seán, Liam, Paul O'Connor and Ger Flynn. He gaped at them as they grinned back.

"Lads, what the feck are ye doing here at this time of the night, for Christ's sake are ye all mad?"

"Now then boy, don't you be getting fresh," answered Liam as he started the engine and pulled the van out of the yard onto the road. He put the full headlights on again and speeded up down the narrow country lanes. Con struggled into a seatbelt; travelling at anything more than a snail's pace recently left him feeling nervous. Liam must have sensed his discomfort because he slowed the van down again and kept it that way.

"Where are we going anyway, you bunch of mad feckers?"

"Into enemy territory!"

"Lads, stop fecking about tell me what the story is! Enemy territory where?"

"We're going down the N17, stone walls and the grass is green. We're going down to Knockma Con. We're going to summon the spirits down to help us!"

Con strained round in his seat to look at his friends in the back. "Have you lot lost yer fecking minds? Knockma, that's miles away. And summon what spirits? Have you two been on the funny fags again? Christ, it's like we were seventeen again."

"We're going to ask the gods for some help, boy," whispered Liam to giggles from the rest. And we've got a few cans in the back to help us find our dark side." More laughter. "Someone find this miserable bastard a can, then." A freezing cold can touched Con on the cheek and he jumped. He took the can and looked at it for a second; then he seemed to reach a decision because he ripped the ring-pull off and drank deep, which he followed with a loud belch.

"Fair enough, if you can't beat them!"

At the moderate speed that Liam had decided on it took them what seemed like an age to travel down into County

Galway and out past Headford to Knockma. They travelled in silence, enjoying the companionship of good friends on a crazy night-time adventure. At last they arrived and parked alongside the barrier that marked the way in to the land surrounding the hill. The five men jumped out of the van, and Paul and Ger handed Con a rucksack to wear on his back.

"Christ lads, this thing weighs a ton. A few cans, you said!"

They trudged up the long road past the ruined tower and the tiny cottage and veered left up the pathway. It was dark, but some light from a fingernail moon lit the way. Con looked to his right up the hill; it was fine while they were skirting the woods, but once they got into the trees it would be a nightmare. Briefly the cows came back to him in a vague recollection of his nightmare from earlier that night, and he shook his head and opened his eyes wide in an effort to stay in touch with the waking reality.

Slowly they followed the path round and up, picking their way over submerged roots and fallen branches. The way was trickier now as they moved under the canopy of trees, and they had to tread with care. They would not be able to explain away an injury sustained out here in a hurry. After they had gone through the trees for about a hundred yards, Seán stopped and held up a raised fist, Vietnam war-style. Liam and Paul started laughing. Seán shushed them with mock seriousness and led them up a mouldering slope to the left. There was a stone wall at the top, and Seán led them over a broken bit and through sharp brambles which grew round a large stone structure. Con was not sure if it was a cairn or a ruined building; in the darkness it was impossible to tell.

The others followed Seán as he climbed the stone structure to the top, and each man gasped as he reached the summit and looked out at the view. The countryside was jet black, with occasional security lights outside farmhouses and late night cars providing the only illumination. In the distance they could just make out the monstrous, hulking form of Connemara, and the more they stared at it through the cloying night the more they were convinced it was moving. In another direction the faint light from the moon reflected off Lough Corrib, and the water seemed like a burning silver knife on the horizon.

The freezing air started to get inside their clothes, and the men started to jig about to stay warm. Ger opened his rucksack and pulled out a bottle of whiskey.

"I brought this just in case. I figured the beer would be too cold on a cold night."

"Sure that'll warm us up Ger, nice one!" said Paul as he relieved Ger of the bottle and started to unscrew the cap.

"Here's to us!" he declared as he took a long drag of the whiskey. He coughed and doubled up, wiping his sleeve across his mouth like a saddle-hardened old cowboy. He held the bottle out to Con, who grabbed it round the neck and took a swig. "Here's to victory!"

Liam took it next. "Here's to Pádraicín," and he passed the bottle to Seán without taking a drink.

"To Pádraicín," said Seán and drank deep from the bottle. He passed it back to Ger, who stood holding the bottle and staring into space.

"What's the matter, Ger, you looking for stars or something?" asked Paul as he tried to pull the bottle out of his hand again.

"Gerroff!" he replied, clutching the bottle to his chest. "I'm trying to think of what to drink to. Err...okay, here's to the Corkman getting us home safely tonight!"

The bottle was passed around amid laughter and spluttering. Con ended up with most of it down his front, because every time he took a swig somebody would make him laugh deliberately. In no time at all the bottle was all but finished, and Ger pulled a lighter and a piece of cloth out of his pocket.

"Right lads," he slurred, "we're going to make a beacon to show these Galway bastards that we've been, and seen and conquered. Or something like that, it was," he mumbled as he tried to arrange the cloth between two stones. The others watched him with nudges and winks.

"What's that cloth, Ger?" asked Liam. "Is that a pair of your jocks? They'll be flammable, sure enough!" The others laughed. "And tell me, what are you trying to do, make a Molotov cocktail or something?"

"But does it look like that, soft lad?" muttered Ger into the collar of his coat. "That would be in the bottle, wouldn't it?" He poured the last drops of whiskey onto the cloth and flicked the lighter. The alcohol started burning with a light made more intense by the darkness. Ger looked up with a huge smile across his face. "Right, now we have to dance round it."

Seán laughed in response. "With drink taken? Are you mad? We'll be all over the place!"

"Yeah, let's just be satisfied we lit a beacon in enemy territory and leave it at that," said Con "Anyway, it's brass monkeys out here. The effects of that whiskey are wearing off fast too." However, Con did not move, hypnotised, like the others, by the dancing flame.

Suddenly a light flutter of dead leaves blew across the flames and rested on the cloth. In a second the leaves were alight and blowing away. The men jerked back to consciousness. "Feck, we'll be burning the wood down!" shouted Con as he leapt after the burning leaves. The others took it in turns to stamp on the whiskey-sodden cloth, trying to put out the burning vapours. "Have we not got any water?" asked Seán as he stamped away. Nobody answered, however, because just as Seán was lifting his foot to bring it down again, the stones under his other foot gave way and he slipped down the side of the huge stone structure, landing with a thud on the rocky ground at the bottom.

"Okay, that's it!" shouted Con as he came round the bottom of the stone mound. "I got the leaves; did you guys get the cloth? Seán, are you alright? Okay then, time to go. That's enough damage for one night! What are we like, it's like we were kids again! And I'm not going back through those brambles again! There's got to be another way down."

They picked Seán up off the floor and trooped round the mound to go down the other side. The going was rough, and although there were no trees, the ground was full of rocks. They had been walking for some distance without really knowing where they were when Con, who was leading the way, let out a shout. "We've come too far, it's a fence. A tall one, at that."

Suddenly all Hell broke loose. Bright floodlights came on with an audible click and dogs started barking from what seemed like every direction. "Feck!" said Con. "It must be the quarry!"

The five men tried to pick their way through the rocks, using the fence as a guide. The dogs found them quickly and jumped at the other side of the fencing.

"Feck!" whimpered Ger. "I bet they can clear that fence. And I bet they're hungry!"

"You know, it doesn't really matter, this quarry belongs to the Mortimers' da," shouted Paul over the noise the dogs were making.

"Try telling that to the dogs. Or to the gards, for that matter," panted Liam.

Finally, with a few scrapes, and much more sober than they had been half an hour before, they found the road, and followed it round to where they had left the van. By the time they were all buckled in they were all helpless with laughter and as they put dark miles between them and Knockma, the story, now an anecdote, grew in exaggeration and length until they hardly recognised it themselves.

When Con finally crawled back into bed it was almost dawn. Deirdre mumbled in her sleep and turned over to move away from Con's freezing cold body. Con lay on his back in the dark tried to catch at least an hour before dawn would put an end to his night.

CHAPTER TWENTY-TWO

For Con, the next two weeks were like waiting for Christmas when he was a child. You knew something special was coming and you could imagine many things about the day, but whatever tricks you tried the day would not come any faster. As a child he had even tried going to bed earlier in an effort to make the next day come more quickly, although he was fast disabused of that idea when he found himself lying in bed, wide awake, waiting in vain for sleep to come and listening with increasing frustration to his family still having fun downstairs.

He trained as usual, and there was no shortage of work to do, either around the farm or in the house, but the time would just not cooperate. There were diversions in the shape of visits from journalists to talk about his involvement in the revival of the championship, but even this brought him no satisfaction. Talkative and outgoing around the people with whom he felt comfortable, Con turned into a shy, monosyllabic lummock whenever a stranger started asking questions.

He resorted to trying to forget that the match was going to take place at all, until the evening in the pub that Liam Murphy reminded them all about the referee from the fateful senior club final. The comments brought the intense feeling of injustice back to him and only served to heighten his desire to beat the men from Galway.

He spoke to the other players about the problem and found them all to be perfectly calm. "It's just you, Con, you need to calm down, lad," they replied with smiles, knowing full well that this reply would only wind him up even more. Of course, the final straw came when reading the comments of various Galway players in the press. Whether or not the comments were taken out of context, or whether they were simply a gross exaggeration, they were enough to send Con's stress levels sky high. Never before had he been so up for it as now.

THESE GREEN FIELDS

At last, after many sleepless nights, the day of the final dawned. Con lay in bed, exhausted, wondering where he was going to suddenly acquire the energy to get up and play the most important game of his career. When he managed to drag himself out of bed he glanced out of the window. It was a grey Irish day, all the colours blending and blurring with an Impressionist attractiveness that insults no intelligence. He packed his things into a bag, kissed Deirdre and the kids goodbye with a 'see you there' and moped round to Seán's for some breakfast and sympathy. Ciara made him a fry which he couldn't eat, to the benefit of Seán's oldest who hovered like a fly around the table waiting for bits of bacon rind and sausage.

In the car on the way to Castlebar for the coach he was not much more communicative, but seeing all the other players and hearing the early morning banter lifted his spirits. He had always enjoyed this the most, right from the word go in his playing career, the buzz of being on the coach, of being one of the chosen few. It still pleased him now and he believed he could trace it back to his childhood, to the joy of being picked, of belonging. Conversation on the coach revolved around the rather strange original decision to play the game in Carraroe. They were no Dutch soccer team; if Galway wanted to play the game in a wild place then Mayo had its fair share of forgotten corners. The players joked about dragging the aristocratic

Galway team up to Tragagh and making them change in the shade of a bus. Perhaps a smaller venue was meant to show the event a certain amount of disdain, as if granting them the honour of playing at Pearse Stadium would lend the Mayo team more credibility than their results deserved. For all the joking though, they were pleased of the change of venue; such a big match deserved a big stadium and a huge crowd.

They arrived early in Salthill, but already the crowds were out in force dressed in the maroon and white of Galway. The people looked up at the red and green-decorated coach as it inched its way along the coast road, and young lads came right up to the bus to wave their flags up at the windows. The Mayo players laughed and joked as they looked out at the crowds, but there was an undeniable nervousness underlying their banter. They had arrived in enemy territory, and they all knew that this game would be nothing like the two qualifiers. On a bad day Galway would play with them, and if they wanted to would put them to the sword.

The bus pulled up to Pearse Stadium, and the players filed out, each man looking at the darkening sky a moment before ducking into the back door and trooping down the narrow corridor to the dressing rooms. The Kilbruagh players looked at each other as they claimed their spots on the bench around the walls. They had been here just a year earlier for the club final against Kinglen, and the memories were coming flooding back.

"Don't think about it, lads," urged Seán, captain for the day. "Today is another day, this is another contest, and we can't believe we're beaten already by something that's in the past."

The team went out onto the pitch to soak up the early atmosphere, and commented on the possibility of rain. While they were out there the Galway boys came out to inspect the stadium too. The two teams mixed for a moment, with players who knew each other from club clashes greeting each other with smiles and others shaking hands and offering comments on the result, before the Mayo team went back down the tunnel to their dressing room.

They changed slowly, laughing and joking and listening to the stand filling up above their heads. They could hear the feet of hundreds of supporters filing in and taking their seats, and the noise was building to a peak. With fifteen minutes left the players made last-minutes adjustments to helmets and gloves and checked their hurls one last time. The bainisteoir walked in to see that all was well, and was greeted with shouts of 'speech!' from the players.

"Feck off lads, who the feck do you think I am, Nell McCafferty? Seán, you say something if you want to."

THESE GREEN FIELDS

Seán looked round at the faces of his team-mates and got slowly to his feet. He had no idea what to say but he trusted that words were about to come out of his mouth. They did indeed.

"Now then lads, this is it, this is the final you all dreamed of playing. This is your chance of glory. In seventy-odd minutes the chance will have gone, and you'll look back and wonder where it went. So now's the moment to think to yourselves, do I want this badly enough? Do I want to go out there and win this? And ask yourselves, why do I want this? Why am I playing this game today? What am I playing for?" The banging of feet on the ceiling was growing louder by the second; the fans obviously knew that the dressing rooms were directly underneath. It was like the Roman coliseum, the public of Rome baying for the gladiators' blood. Seán continued talking to the players. "We are from a beautiful land, and that's what we're playing for today. We're playing for our own green fields, the land of Granuaile and Cromwell's damnation and the coffin ships. And on those ships, these green fields are what they sang about, what they longed to see again and never did." The banging grew to a crescendo, a uniform tattoo like the beating of a drum, or the beating of the players' hearts, the sound of gunfire. "But we're not playing for our lives, or even for land or food, we're playing for pride and honour. The same

pride and honour that made our fathers and grandfathers fight
for what they believed in on these green fields. So let's go and
make our fathers and grandfathers proud."

The banging was in their heads now, and as Seán hit
their hurls with his and stared into their eyes, the Mayo players
jumped up and shouted back at him. Yes! Let's go and win
this! Come on lads!

*Welcome to Pearse Stadium in beautiful Galway, and
the final of, what is this though, is this the final of the Connacht
Senior Hurling Championship, Pat? – Well, you tell me
Mickey, and good afternoon to all our viewers, and indeed
welcome to Galway for what proves to be an exciting tie
whatever it is they are playing for. – Yes indeed, Pat whatever
it is they are going to win today the players are well up for this
and as we've heard over the last fortnight talking to the players
on both teams this is as important a match as any of them are
likely to play in a while. One thing is certain, though, titles
aside, the crowd will definitely be the winners today because
this game promises to be the game of the year, the All-Ireland
aside, certainly in this part of the country.*

The team ran down the corridor, into the tunnel, out
onto the pitch to the roars of thirty thousand people, and stood
in a mob near the halfway line waiting for the fight. The crowd
sang as one and waved their banners, savouring their own

atmosphere. The Mayo players fidgeted nervously, anxious to maintain their own high until the match started, but the Galway team were going to do their own thing. They waited for as long as they could before trotting calmly out onto the pitch. It's just another game. We do this all the time. No pressure.

And the teams are out! The Mayo team looked so psyched there, but the Galway players seem to have almost sauntered onto the pitch. Cocky, would you say? – No, they have to be confident though, don't they. – So Pat, a prediction? – Well Mickey, it's too tight to call, you know, in spite of the theoretical superiority of Galway hurling this Mayo side are an excellent team. – Although they made a hames of the League earlier in the year. – Ah now, that's a little unfair, Mickey if I may say so. – You may. – You know I thought they were unlucky against Wicklow, and they only lost to Kildare by the one point so they were in it until the end there. – Okay Pat, but can they do it today against this Galway side? – Well the players would never admit to this, they always have to display the same amount of commitment whatever the game and whoever the opposition, but let's face it, this is the auld enemy they're playing against and it's inevitable that they're going to up their game for this one. Then of course there's the little rivalries they bring into the game from club level too, you remember the Senior Club clash between Kilbruagh of Mayo and Kinglen of Galway, very controversial and of course we have five Kilbruagh players in the Mayo side today, do you think they will remember that defeat? – I'm sure they will, Mickey, and if they don't, some player will remind them of it on the pitch I'm sure.

A watched pot never boils, but when you turn away it will bubble and steam. The Mayo players had just decided to copy the Galway players in knocking up in front of their own fans when the referee called the forwards over. Con realised that even though their own high may have been deflated by the wait, Galway's apparent nonchalance could go against them too. If Mayo started the brighter, they could take some early points, and in a game as unpredictable as this a few points could make all the difference come full time.

We look like we're under way now, Pat as the players step forward and the referee throws in and we're off! The clash of the ash and the ball falls to the Galway side, picked up there in midfield and Galway mount the first attack of the half, out of midfield to the half-forward line, Mayo defending from the front and not letting Galway find a way through, very intense the opening stages here at the Pearse Stadium, Galway, and that's a little too intense and it's going to be a free. Do you think he'll try it from there? And he does, and it's the first point of the afternoon for the home side. Mayo starting

153

strongly there but Galway taking their first chance with cool heads.

The game continued with more Galway attacks, and all of Mayo's efforts to stop them appeared to end either in frees or at least in some angry clash of hurls which the referee could not penalise but did nothing to help the atmosphere on the pitch. The crowd sensed this and the shouts grew louder and angrier; the sky frowned down and threatened to join in. Con and Seán tried to calm their players down enough to play more sensibly, but they knew only too well that in the heat of battle there was no way to get red-blooded hurlers to act rationally or calm down.

Galway surged forward again and again and the points started to accumulate and the Mayo team became more and more frustrated, lashing out with their hurls or trying sneaky trips and pulls of the shirt. Mayo needed something to help them settle or the game would run away with them. The chance came with twenty minutes gone and Galway leading already by five points. The Galway right half-forward took one knock too many and turned on Paul O'Connor, the Mayo left half-back. At such close range the pushing and shoving would never be anything more than a playground skirmish, and as a dozen more players joined in the melee it was too much of a squash for anybody to get hurt, but it enabled the referee to get in and take control of the situation. As the two captains pulled their players away the referee called some of them aside for a talking to, and the angry exchange was defused.

So Pat, the first scrap of the game, and it was coming for some time, what do you say? – I agree, Mickey, the way the Mayo players were handling the pressure it was inevitable that somebody would take a swing back. – So you think the pressure's telling on the Mayo lads, then? – Well, you can see that Galway are all over them there for long periods and Mayo can't seem to handle it, they're not getting the tackles in and they're trying to substitute them with a more aggressive approach, and aggression's good but they have to keep their temper too. One thing's hustling and another's just hitting the players. – And I can't see where Mayo are going to get their attacks from either, every time Galway get a point and Mayo get the ball they waste it, they just give it straight back. – Yes, but know I think this little scuffle will benefit Mayo more. The pushing and shoving will have allowed them to blow off a little steam and hopefully the break in play will allow them to regroup and think about what they're trying to do. They won't have got this far to want to just throw it away now, will they?

Down on the pitch Seán was grabbing players and hissing urgently in their ears before almost throwing them back into their positions. He was obviously thinking the same as the commentators and was attempting to rein in the team in before the game was beyond their reach. Whatever he was hissing at them seemed to have the desired effect, though, because during the next ten minutes they held Galway back at every turn and the home team failed to increase their lead. Then with minutes to go before half time Ger Flynn put two points over without reply and Mayo were back within a goal of their neighbours. Thirty seconds left and Mayo broke down the right with a tremendous hit from Paul O'Connor, bypassing midfield and straight for the forward line. Con challenged for the ball inside the twenty-metre line and won it; turning sharply he went for the posts.

So it's half time and Mayo have somehow managed to claw their way back into the game with three uncontested points there right at the end, so it's Galway who lead by twelve points to ten. – And that sets things up nicely for the second half, I was worried for a little while there Mickey, you know I hate it when a game's over by half time, it gives you nothing to look forward to for the rest of the afternoon. – I agree totally, Pat, I like my hurling to last seventy minutes too, and a few more if I can grab them, thirty-five minutes isn't enough for anybody with a real appetite for a contest. So the second half then, which way will it swing, do you think? – It's going to go right to the wire, I think, Mick, so Galway need to keep putting

*those points over like they were doing in the first twenty
minutes or so and Mayo have to keep plugging away, not let
the opposition get under their skin, just keep pushing and
taking their chances too. – But I must press you for a
prediction, Pat we can't leave our viewers hanging. – Then I'll
say either Galway or Mayo, by a small margin. – Thank you,
Pat, you've certainly come down off the fence there.*

Down in the dressing room the Mayo team munched
on bananas and adjusted their gloves. Rather than do another
full-blown speech, the bainisteoir and the captain went round
the players individually and said quiet words. Keep in there,
keep pushing, take the points, remember the training. Nothing
negative, no accusations, the game's not lost. The physio
rubbed muscles and passed round water bottles. Time to go,
and the players jumped up as if they were starting all over
again, as if they had not just played thirty-five long, hard
minutes.

Out on the pitch the scene had changed. The sky had
darkened so much that the floodlights had had to be turned on,
and it looked like the rain would start at any moment. In the
stand the crowd huddled together to escape the early winter
weather and the terraces were a sea of gaudy umbrellas in
anticipation of the downpour.

THESE GREEN FIELDS

The referee threw in and the game started where it had left off, with Mayo appearing to have the better of the play, especially in front of the posts. They drew level, and then went a point ahead. The Galway skipper had to rally his own troops now; they could not lose this game. They were behind for the first time, and at an important point. The home team pushed forward and levelled the scores again.

Backwards and forwards went the score, first one team up and then the other. Con was playing his heart out, flying in for every challenge. Seán threw him occasional worried glances; he would always have Con on his side on any team he played for, but there was also a little voice in the back of his head that constantly took him back to the injury. It was the little voice that Con had feared before he had come back and apparently could not hear. Seán valued his passion, but he knew how scared he had been when his friend had been on the operating table.

Now the rain came, long lazy sheets that swept everything and everyone forward in its merciless embrace. In seconds all the players were soaked, their shirts clinging to their skin and their shorts sticking to their legs. The hurls became unpredictable in their hands; the ground was treacherous. As the game got wetter, the points dried up, with all the play confined to the growing quagmire in the middle of the park. Whenever anybody managed to get a shot off – more from frustration than from any real scoring chance – the ball flew wide if it even reached the posts at all.

Now the players have a common enemy they seem less inclined to clash among themselves, Pat. – Yes, I agree and with fifty minutes gone, the game seems to have lost its way a little. I'm not sure what it'll take to kick start it again though, although the rain and wind could certainly stop for me.

Visibility was reduced to barely the next line of players as the rain sheeted across the pitch, and the players were growing frustrated as they had in the first half as ball after ball went astray. The tackles were becoming harder by the minute and everyone could see there was a danger of another flare-up. Mayo could not afford another fight now; the referee would not be as lenient as in the first half, and they were still only just clinging on. All Galway needed was a half-chance to put some daylight between the teams on the scoreboard and it would be all over.

And the game was about to take a turn for the worse.

The ball came over to Con on the right, and he attempted a run with the slíotar seemingly stuck to his hurl in the rain. The Galway left corner-back decided this was the time for decisive action and threw himself into a shoulder barge that not only knocked Con off kilter, it sent him sliding off the pitch. The Mayo man accelerated as he flew over the relatively smooth grass in the corner and crashed into the advertising hoardings with a sickening smash. His hurl flew up in the air and came to rest in the crowd. The supporters in the corner leaned over to have a look at the unfortunate player then recoiled as they saw the new shape of Con's arm.

Seán saw the supporters straighten up from across the pitch; he saw their expressions change from excited to disgusted, and knew in an instant that Con was seriously hurt. He ran across the pitch just as the bainisteoir sent the physios on, and when he arrived he found Con squirming with the pain of a dislocated shoulder.

"For feck's sake, Con, this was no time to be taking up the luge!"

Con snorted out a laugh as he tried to sit up, but the effort was too much and he lay back down in the puddle which had formed in the angle of the pitch and the hoarding. The physios arrived and a Galway supporter leaned across the barrier to hand Con's hurl to Seán. Seán turned to look across the pitch, and through the incessant sheets of rain he could see the bainisteoir yelling instructions into the ear of a substitute. He looked back down at Con anxiously; they needed Con on the pitch, but if he was unable to carry on there was nothing they could do. Unfortunately it would be another story entirely convincing Con of this. He had just come back from one serious injury, and to make it this far through a championship final only to lose out to another injury would be too much for his proud, obstinate friend.

A shout from behind him brought him back to the game. The referee had allowed play to continue because the injured player was off the pitch. Seán had to get back on and play. For a second he tried to think of something to say to Con, but his mind was in game mode and nothing appropriate came into it, so he lay the hurl down by Con's side, turned and trotted back out into the final. Con saw him go and turned his head to try and see what was happening without him, but the pain was too intense and he gave in to the quick, professional hands of the physios. It was game over for him.

And what a resounding smash that was for Con O'Coolahan, Pat, and a terrible blow for his team too. – Yes, Mick, there's no way back from there, I reckon, Galway have to take advantage of the fact that one of Mayo's best players is off the pitch. Mayo are leading by one but there's still nearly fifteen minutes left, that's more than enough time for Galway to take this game by the scruff and shake it until everything falls out of its pockets. – Nicely put, Pat, can Mayo hang on though? Is there still a game for the ten or so minutes that are left? –

There's still a game, but you have to say at this point that Galway have the advantage.

With the Mayo team still trying to reorganise itself on the pitch after the loss of Con and the introduction of a new player, Galway quickly drew level and started to press home the psychological advantage they had gained. Mayo hung on with grim determination, pressuring the Galway players while trying desperately not to give away a free. Inside the last ten minutes, and Galway somehow started to increase the pace of the game. Thanks only to the state of the pitch, which was becoming increasingly unplayable with the amount of rain, Mayo kept the forwards occupied outside of shooting range, but they could not hold on forever.

Con watched from the sidelines, helpless as his team-mates repelled wave after wave of opposition attacks. The physios had helped him to his feet, and were now trying to walk him round the pitch to the tunnel, but the player was far more interested in what was happening on the pitch to care about his injury. The shoulder could wait, and Con was playing every single ball alongside his team. The pain was excruciating – even the rain falling on his shoulder seemed to burn like molten lava – but he knew the pain of defeat lasted a lot longer.

Five minutes to go and yet another Galway attack saw the forward free himself of his marker in front of goal, and he was not going to score an easier point all afternoon. Galway were ahead by one, and the maroon-clad supporters in the main stand breathed out in a collective gasp of relief. They were ahead, and with some decent defending from the front they should stay that way. The Mayo players were on the ropes now, and a desperate lunge from Ger Flynn, defending with the rest of the team, made him lose his balance and crash into the Galway player. Harsh, but the referee gave the free. Galway were two up.

What are Mayo going to do now? Where are they going to find that last push to take them across the line? Two down, just minutes remaining, and it looks like heartbreak for the men from Mayo. – But how many times have we seen that, Pat, one team has stayed in it all the way but really there's only one team in it, and that team has to make its quality show at the end, to go that bit further and hit that bit harder, that's what makes a champion team, and you have to say it, even though Mayo have fought well, Galway are a champion team. – But it's not over yet, as the Galway supporters sing in the stands with their team two up, a goal could change this totally, although really nobody's troubled either keeper today, especially since the rain started, but now it's Mayo, starting from their half-back line, bringing it up the wing, Galway forcing them wide, keeping them under control with just two minutes to go, the game is theirs for the winning, Liam Murphy up the wing to Ger Flynn who's moved outside to try and cover the absence of Con O'Coolahan, he twists and he turns, he's trying to find a way in there but he's two men on him, there's no way through for him, he keeps trying, and oh, that's a beautiful piece of hurling! That was sensational hurling with seventy minutes of hard running in his legs he's kept the ball balanced on the hurl and he pucks the ball back over his head and ducks through the wall set up by the Galway players, manages to stay on his feet in spite of their best intentions and will he go for the posts? Is there time to go for points now or must it be a goal? He puts the ball into the middle, looking for Seán O'Flaherty.

CHAPTER TWENTY-THREE

And he finds Seán O'Flaherty, and he is going for goal, he's going for glory, he's seen a gap and he swings his hurl as if his life depended on it. Oh Mickey, oh Mickey, oh Mickey!

CHAPTER TWENTY-FOUR

And that's a goal! No! The keeper has got across and has tipped it with his hurl, where's it gone, Mickey? Tell me where it's gone? Which flag is it? It's white! It's a white flag! O'Flaherty went for goal and somehow, I don't know how he did it, the Galway goalkeeper has got across his goal and flung out an arm and tipped the ball with his hurl and it's dropped over the bar! That's a point, but it's not what Mayo wanted or needed, and now Galway come back and there's going to be no time for any more, that's it! It's over, and what a dramatic end we've seen, and Mayo won't thank me for saying this, but what better end could you possibly ask for to a game of hurling!

CHAPTER TWENTY-FIVE
December

Con sat slumped in his armchair, staring blindly through the window. His boys had already been at it with the fake snow and hardly anything could be seen of the small garden outside, but Con was not interested in what was happening in the real world. In his mind he was replaying the game, going over and over his injury and the missed points, and that incredible, unbelievable save by the Galway stopper. He did not hear the door open or Deirdre's words, and it was only when Seán sat down heavily in the other armchair that he realised he was no longer alone.

He obliged himself to look across at Seán and acknowledge him, breaking the spell that solitude had woven in his mind. Seán had a hurl across his lap, and he was sat smiling over at his friend.

"So, how's that arm then?"

Con raised his elbow as far as he could in the sling. "Getting better. I can almost move it normally."

"How long have you got?"

"Another two weeks, I reckon, the doctor said three."

"That must have hurt," said Seán with a wince.

"Not as much as seeing that ball drop over the bar. That will stay with me for a long time, will that one." He shook his head and looked away, the pain evident in his eyes. Seán looked down at the carpet and traced the pattern with his eyes. He had gone through the same moment in his head a thousand times in the last week, trying to make the slíotar go into the top corner of the goal, but every time the images blanked out just before the ball reached the line. You could not change history. And they had almost made history. He sighed, and Con turned his head to look at him again.

"You feeling it too?"

"Yeah, I can't get that shot out of me head."

"Me neither. Seán, I swear I don't know what to do."

"With what, Con?"

"The hurling. Right now I never want to step on that pitch for as long as I live. But another part of me can't just give up like that. I can't end my career on that defeat. The problem is, will there ever be a victory to take that one away? You can't undefeat a defeat."

Seán stood up and took two steps over to Con's armchair. He laid the hurl gently across his friend's legs, careful not to let the hurl slip down and touch his arm. "That's why I brought you that, my friend. So you could touch it, feel it in your hands again. You know you can't give up, Con. What about next year?"

Con looked up at his friend's face. "Next year, what?"

"What if we get another chance at them?"

Con looked down at the hurl, and started to stroke it with his good hand. He felt the long, smooth shaft of ash and the gracious curves lovingly shaped by a master craftsman. He struggled out of the armchair and stood with the hurl in his hand, staring into Seán's eyes. Then he turned and walked slowly to the living-room door. He stopped and looked round.

"Another chance. That's what life is built on, isn't it Seán, on getting another chance? Well, we'll just have to take that chance next time, won't we?"

Disclaimer:

All of the people included in this story – with the exception of Eddie Brennan's brief cameo appearance and a mention of the Mortimer family – are fictional creations. Any names which may exist in reality are the result of coincidence.

Some of the places and institutions (for example the GAA, the Mayo board of selectors, Croke Park, various counties and the Atlantic Ocean) are taken from real life; however there is no intentional resemblance to reality and any similarities are purely coincidental.

Apologies:

My apologies to both Portumna GAA club and Ballina James Stephens for unceremoniously removing them from the 2007 Connacht SHC final in favour of my own fictional clubs.

As for Laois and Westmeath trying to join Ulster – this was not an attempt on my part to create controversy. Please remember that this is, after all, a work of fiction!